BEAUTY IN DARKNESS

ROYAL HEARTS BOOK ONE

ELIZABETH BRIGGS

For Erin, the light that came from darkness

ONE

ROSE

The wizard arrived at dusk, appearing from the shadows as if conjured by the very darkness settling over the forest. One moment there was nothing before me but ice hanging from the barren branches of a tree, the next, dark tendrils swirled like smoke, slowly forming the body of a man. A very tall man, with hair as black as a raven's wing, a regal face that seemed to be carved from pure stone, and cold eyes that narrowed as soon as they saw me.

A strange wizard this near the castle meant trouble, especially one who could teleport. I shot to my feet, raising my hand to trace a rune in the air. "Who are you? What are you doing here?"

He gave my silvery rune a look of pure disdain as it hovered beside me, flickering like fading candlelight. "Is that supposed to stop me?"

I finished the rune and it flared brighter before vanishing, conjuring a long spear of ice in its place. "Get back, or I'll be forced to attack!"

"I'd prefer if you didn't." The wizard swept aside his cloak and took a step forward into the secluded clearing where I stood. "But do what you must."

His nonchalant tone threw me off, as did his refined voice and fine clothes. He wore all black, with silver thread woven into the edges of the fabric, and his boots were polished to perfection. He towered over me, and a shiver of fear ran down my spine at the power emanating from him. More power than I had ever encountered before. But he had entered my forest without warning, and I wouldn't back down.

I kept the spear of ice hovering in the air, pointed at his chest. "What do you want?"

"I'm here to speak with King Balsam." His arrogant gaze assessed me and seemed to find me lacking in some way. "And you are?"

I lifted my chin and held his eye. "Prepared to stop you."

An eyebrow lifted. "I'd like to see you try."

I flicked my wrist and the ice shard shot toward him. He traced a rune of his own, so fast the silvery light flashed through the air for only an instant. My ice spear turned to water and splashed all over my gown, chilling me immediately. My mouth fell open as I glanced down at the cold, wet fabric clinging to my legs.

At that moment I realized who he was—and how foolish I'd been to think I could have used magic to stop him. There were few wizards powerful enough to teleport, fewer still who were bold enough to use magic against a princess of Talador, and only one who matched his description. "You're King Raith of Ilidan," I said, my voice barely above a whisper.

"Indeed." He tilted his head as he examined me. "Am I allowed to know your name now?"

My cheeks burned, but I squared my shoulders and faced him without flinching. "I'm Princess Rose, second daughter of King Balsam."

"Ah." He took another step closer, his eyes locked with mine. "Tell me, Princess, what does your father think of you using magic? I thought he had forbidden it in Talador."

My lips pressed into a thin line and I didn't respond. He already knew the answer. My mother's old spellbook sat on the small stone bench behind me, where I'd been practicing before he'd arrived and disrupted me.

"Oh, but of course he doesn't know," Raith continued. "That must be why you hide out here in the shadow of the palace with none but the forest knowing your secrets." He leaned forward and lowered his voice. "Don't worry. I won't tell either."

The man standing far too close to me was a monster, by all accounts. I should have been terrified or angered by his presence here. I should have run to alert the guards or shouted for help. But I did none of those things, and found I couldn't look away from the darkly captivating man who loomed over me.

I'd heard many tales of the dreaded wizard king, my kingdom's greatest enemy, the man my father feared and hated more than anyone else in the Six Kingdoms. They said he sacrificed animals for his dark magic, that he could wipe out entire battalions of soldiers with deadly spells, and that he'd given his soul to the Shadow Lord in exchange for power. There were rumors he'd taken his throne from his mother by force, and that his wife had killed herself to escape his cruelty. I wasn't sure if any of those stories were true, but they all agreed on one thing—King Raith was a man to be feared.

I should have recognized him immediately, but I'd never thought we would actually meet in person, and certainly not in the middle of the forest. In my defense, he was younger than I'd expected him to be...and far more handsome. Dark and magnetic, his presence commanded attention and his eyes missed nothing. They were the color of a storm about to turn dangerous, filled with hidden power and ready to strike —much like the rest of him.

"Why do you want to speak with my father?" I asked.

"To end this war between our kingdoms. It's gone on far too long." His voice was colder than the snow under my feet, despite his words of peace. I wondered what he would ask of my father in return for ending hostilities. Talador and Ilidan had been at war for decades, since long before I was born, and the cost of the endless standoff was high. When Raith became king a few years ago, it had only gotten worse. With his magic and formidable army, we were losing ground every day against Ilidan and the war was bankrupting our kingdom and forcing our people to starve. Surely my father would agree to whatever Raith wanted, knowing we couldn't continue on this path any longer. Not without losing far too many lives.

Then again, my father cared little for reason or empathy these days, so it was hard to know what he would do. I'd been told he was a good man before my mother passed away, but I'd never seen that side of him. And with each year, he only became colder. Would he do what was best for our kingdom, or would his pride make him continue this never-ending war?

"I'll take you to him." If I brought Raith to the castle there might be less of a panic from his sudden, unexpected arrival. Or so I hoped.

He idly waved my offer away. "No need. I'd prefer to make an entrance."

"If that's so, why teleport out here in the middle of nowhere and not closer to the castle?"

"Despite your father's hatred of magic, the castle's wards still stand and they prevent me from teleporting anywhere near it. I could break through them of course, but why spend the energy?" He gave a casual shrug, dripping with haughty confidence. "Good evening, Princess Rose."

His gaze dropped to my gown, which had begun to freeze against my legs, and heat spread through me as his eyes lingered there. An instant later the fabric was dry and warm, as if it had been sitting under the sun for an hour. I was so startled I could only stare back at him, wondering how he'd done it. I'd heard tales that the best wizards could perform magic without casting runes, that they formed the intricate lines and symbols in their minds and that was enough, but I'd never encountered such a thing before. Until now.

He gave me a quick nod and then set off, his boots crunching through the snow and his black cloak flowing behind him. He brought to mind an image of a raven in flight, and I couldn't help but stare after him as he disappeared from sight between the dense trees.

I quickly grabbed my mother's spellbook and wrapped my heavy cloak around me, shivering against the chill. The sun had vanished below the horizon, and with it the last traces of warmth in the air. Even so, it was only autumn. Talador would soon get much colder, and unlike Raith, I couldn't teleport away.

I hurried after the wizard king in the direction he'd gone, but didn't see any trace of him in the frost-covered, empty forest. Cursing myself for not riding a horse out here, or at least bringing a torch, I trudged through the snow in the increasing darkness, my skirts snagging on branches that seemed intent on slowing me down. Part of the wizard king's magic, or simply a sign I'd lost track of time and been out here longer than I should? I wasn't sure.

As I climbed the hill, the gleaming white castle rose before me between the pine trees. With majestic pointed towers and shining spires that reached high into the sky, Winton Castle appeared as if it had been formed from ice, and it overlooked the snow-covered forest and the capital of Ralston like a sentinel.

I quickened my pace and found the castle already in a state of upheaval by the time I entered its large gates.

Guards stood on high alert, servants rushed past me in a panic, and every voice seemed to mention the wizard king's arrival. From snippets of overheard conversation I learned he'd arrived surrounded by darkness with lightning crackling in his palms, and had demanded to see my father immediately. He'd been escorted to the throne room by a contingent of wary soldiers, and rumors were flying about what was happening now behind those closed doors.

I moved quickly through the castle's pale halls decorated with thick tapestries and blazing torches to fight back the constant chill. My older sister Lily found me in the corridor leading to our bedrooms, her ever-present guard Keane walking stiffly a pace behind her. They made a striking pair, both tall, serious, and attractive, except she had the same long, dark hair as I did, while his was a dark gold that contrasted nicely with his blue and white armor.

"Rose!" Lily said, as she approached me. "Where have you been? King Raith of Ilidan has arrived with no advance notice whatsoever. Can you believe it?"

"I know," I said, as I continued toward my room. "We met."

"You did?" She glanced at me sharply and missed a step on the lush carpet, nearly stumbling. Somehow I'd managed to surprise my always stoic sister. "When? How?"

I pushed open my bedroom door and we slipped inside, while Keane crossed his arms and waited in the hall. A fire already burned in the hearth, bringing some warmth to the otherwise cold stone room filled with my bed, wardrobe, dresser, and a small desk. The heavy fabrics were all embroidered with pink and white roses, as befit my name.

"In the clearing where I practice," I said, once I was sure we were alone.

Lily's blue eyes dipped to where I'd tucked our mother's spellbook inside my cloak, and a frown crossed her lips. "What happened?"

I set the book on the dresser and removed my cloak, which was coated in a thin sheen of ice. "He appeared in front of me, we shared a few words, and I foolishly attacked him with magic. He said he wanted to speak with Father, and then he left for the castle. That was all."

Her eyes widened. "He saw you use magic?"

"Yes, but I doubt he will tell Father. It would be rather hypocritical of him, after all."

She sat on the edge of my bed and watched me with a worried gaze. "Still, I don't like that he knows, and I wish you wouldn't keep this up. If Father finds out..."

"He won't. Even if he did, I won't ever stop. It's my only connection to her." My fingers lightly ran over the embossed cover of the old leather spellbook, the one thing I owned of our mother's. Lily likely had the gift too since it ran in families, but she'd never tried to learn magic. Unlike me, Lily always followed the rules. She was the perfect daughter and royal heir in every way, much to our father's delight. And me? I was the daughter he wanted to forget, whose eyes he could never meet, whom he wished had never been born.

"What was King Raith like?" Lily asked. "Was he as horrible as they say? Were you scared at all?"

"He was rather brooding and intense, and his magic was impressive. But no, I wasn't scared." Perhaps I should have been, but I'd never felt I was in danger while in his presence. He could have easily killed me with the slightest thought, especially after I'd attacked him, but instead he'd dried my gown so I wouldn't freeze out there. "He was younger than I expected too."

Lily nodded. "He took the throne two years ago, when he was only twenty-three."

Barely older than Lily then, who was twenty-two, and one year my elder. I couldn't imagine being crowned so young. No wonder he was so serious.

Iris, our youngest sister, burst into the room and asked, "Is it true? Is the wizard king here?"

"It's true," Lily said. "He says he's come in peace, though no one believes it. He's speaking with Father now."

"He told me he wants to end the war," I said, as I moved around the room to light some candles.

"Did he? Why now, I wonder?" Lily shook her head. "I'm not sure if Father will welcome him or send him away, but I've ordered a feast tonight in King Raith's honor anyway, though the staff aren't happy about it. I can't blame them, honestly. Who simply arrives unannounced like that?" She let out a little shudder. It was just like Lily to be more horrified by King Raith's lack of social graces than the fact that our kingdom's most dangerous foe had arrived at our front door with deadly magic dripping from his fingertips.

Iris sat on the bed next to Lily, her legs swinging off the

ground. "I heard he cast lightning at the guards and struck them all down. I wonder if he would teach us magic too?"

"Definitely not," Lily said in her firm, oldest sister voice. She leveled a look at me that clearly said *this is all your doing*. "And he didn't strike anyone down."

"Too bad. I would have liked to see that." Iris hopped off the bed, headed over to my spellbook, and flipped it open. Like me, she had the gift, although it wouldn't be fully available to her until she reached puberty. "But you'll teach me, won't you Rose?"

"Maybe when you're older." I ruffled her red hair, and she pulled away with a scowl that only managed to look adorable on her twelve-year-old face.

Lily sighed and shook her head as she rose to her feet. She wasn't opposed to magic like our father, she simply worried about us crossing him. "Come, Iris. Let's get ready for the feast. If all goes well, perhaps you can meet the wizard king yourself."

Iris perked up at that. "Can I wear your icicle tiara?"

"Yes, but only if you promise to be extra careful with it," Lily said, as the two of them left the room.

I closed the door after them and wondered if our other sisters were getting ready as well. There were six of us total from four different mothers, all of us named after flowers as was the custom for the royal family of Talador. Lily was the eldest and the future queen, while I was the second daughter and reluctant spare. Jasmine loved the outdoors and was a fine archer, Camellia would rather be a guard than a princess, her twin Violet always had her nose in a book, and Iris was perhaps even more headstrong and rebellious than me.

Yes, our father had four marriages, though none of his wives lasted long after becoming queen. Lily and I came from his first marriage, Jasmine from his second, the twins from his third, and Iris from the last. We'd long wondered if our father would take another bride, but so far he hadn't. A good thing too because she likely would have been about my age, and that would have been far too awkward.

I turned to my wardrobe and studied my gowns, debating which to wear this evening for the feast. I wanted to look bold and fearless when facing King Raith again, to show him I wasn't afraid of him revealing my secret. My blood red gown, perhaps. The one with the low neckline, flared skirt, and black trim. I held it up to me in the mirror, my hands running along the smooth crimson velvet. Yes, perfect. He wouldn't be able to keep his eyes off me all night.

I wasn't sure why that mattered, but it did.

TWO

RAITH

L arge, ornate double doors opened wide to reveal Talador's throne room, a long stretch of stark white stone with high ceilings and thick, embellished columns. At the far end, King Balsam sat on the Frozen Throne with a view of the frost-covered forest behind him. The throne was made of crystal, despite its name, and was styled to look like shards of ice were splintering off from the chair. King Balsam was draped in heavy furs and wore a large silver and sapphire crown atop his head. Despite only being in his mid-forties—younger than my parents, had they still been alive—his hair was stark white and his face was heavily lined.

He sat up at the sight of me and his icy voice boomed out from his throne. "King Raith of Ilidan. You have some nerve showing up here without invitation. I should have you struck down for even daring to enter my lands. Why are you here?"

I strode down the long, thick carpet without hesitation, while the guards stared at me with open hostility. "I've come to demand that you end the war against my kingdom and remove your soldiers from our borders immediately."

He snorted. "I don't think you're in a position to demand anything."

"Is that so?" I raised my hand as if to draw a rune. "If I were to attack you now, you could stop me?"

"Your sorcery doesn't scare me, Raith."

My eyes narrowed, hatred burning through my veins like poison. "Then perhaps I'll simply end this war by claiming your life."

"Guards!" he shouted, rising to his feet.

A dozen soldiers moved toward me and drew their swords, but I formed a rune in my mind and they all flew back against the wall as if thrown by an invisible catapult. Each one hit the stone hard and crumpled to the floor, where they found themselves unable to move further. Then I leveled my gaze at the King and lifted him five feet into the air, dangling him like a puppet. He let out a choked cry, his eyes bulging.

"You were saying?" I asked.

"Perhaps we can come to some kind of agreement," Balsam gasped.

"Indeed." I released him, and he fell to the marble floor in a heap of furs. "Our kingdoms have been at this tired war for generations, but it's time to end it now."

He slowly sat himself on the throne again, as if moving

was difficult for him now, and the look he gave me was pure malice. "Are you surrendering?"

"No. You are."

A bitter laugh escaped him. "And why would I do that?"

"Because your people are starving, and you have neither the gold nor the stamina to continue this war any longer."

He leaned forward on his throne, gripping the arms tightly. "I've been fighting this war longer than you've been alive, boy. Don't question my stamina."

It took all my effort not to roll my eyes. "This war is pointless. We fight because we have always fought, but that needs to end now. Especially when the threat from Mesner grows every day. We can't afford to fight each other and defend against their army too."

Balsam leaned back and drummed his fingers on the throne's armrest as he considered my words. It was a long time before he spoke, but when he did his voice held less anger. "I've heard their young queen is ambitious. She wishes to rule every one of the Six Kingdoms."

"I've heard the same. Mesner's army has always been the strongest. If they move on us, our kingdoms would be first to fall, weakened as they are already." I had another reason for wanting to end this war as quickly as possible, a threat within my own borders that I needed to address before it destroyed my kingdom from the inside out, but I wasn't about to let Balsam know of such weakness. If he did, he would march on my lands and end this war once and for all, with my people under his oppressive boot. "But if we end the war and stand together as allies, our show of strength might make her hesitate before attacking either of us."

A cold, calculating smile spread across his face. "How desperate you must be if you've come to me, your greatest enemy, for an alliance against Mesner. Would Korelan not help you?"

"They'll stand with me as well, but I would prefer two allies at my back. Or, if nothing else, one less enemy to fight." I took a step forward. "I propose we both remove our soldiers and begin negotiations on the border lands. I'm willing to concede the area of Worth, in exchange for the western part of Hamfit. I'd also like to work out a trade agreement that could benefit us both."

"Hmm." Balsam steepled his fingers and gazed at me with cunning eyes. "What guarantee do I have that you'll remove your soldiers after I remove mine?"

"None but my word."

"Not good enough. I want some kind of reassurance. Something to solidify our new relationship and this potential alliance."

I clenched my fists at the thought of working with this wretched man, but I reminded myself I had to do this to protect my people. "What do you propose?"

He leaned forward on his throne. "An immediate end to the war between our kingdoms, sealed with an alliance through marriage."

"Marriage," I said, my voice flat. I'd known it might come to this, though I'd hoped he would simply see reason and concede defeat. I had no interest in marrying again, especially not to this man's spawn, but a political marriage with one of his daughters would ensure his cooperation and quickly put an end to this needless war. More than that, it would allow me to take something precious from him—as he'd once taken from me.

"I have six beautiful daughters," Balsam said. "If I give you one of them, would you remove your troops and stand with me against Mesner, should the time come?"

I bowed my head and prayed Silena would forgive me. "I would."

"Then I agree to your terms, King Raith. I too tire of our old war, and we must prepare to face new threats that are now rising. You may take one of my daughters as your bride. You'll meet them all at the feast tonight and can see which one is to your liking then."

"I don't need a feast. Call them forth now so we can get this over with."

"At least let them prepare first," he said, waving a dismissive hand. "Give them some time to make themselves pretty for you."

An image of Princess Rose came forth, from when I'd happened upon her in the forest. Her beauty had been striking, with her long dark hair, smooth skin, and red lips. She had no need to "make herself pretty," as he'd said. She was lovely already, even when fumbling with runes she had no business conjuring. Something about her fierce determination had drawn me to her, so much so that I'd been hesitant to leave the clearing. A longing had stirred in me that I hadn't felt in years, and never wanted to feel again.

Naturally, that was why I could never choose her for my bride. I wasn't sure how I could choose at all, to be honest. None of them would ever compare to what I'd once had and then lost.

"I care not what they look like," I said. "This isn't a love match. Bring them forward and let's be done with it."

"Very well." The King waved a flippant hand and called out, "Summon the princesses."

THREE

A sharp knock sounded on my door while my lady's maid finished doing my hair up in an intricate style. Princess Dahlia—my aunt, and the King's younger sister—stepped inside a moment later, apprehension written all over her face. We had the same dark wavy hair, but she had my father and Lily's ice blue eyes. I'd inherited my mother's eyes, a strange amber color that was common among the wizards of Korelan but rarely seen elsewhere. Iris had inherited similar eyes from her own mother as well.

Dahlia moved to stand behind me, meeting my gaze in the mirror. "Our king has summoned you to the throne room. You must go immediately."

I rose to my feet, unease swirling in my stomach. Had Raith told my father about my magic after all? "Only me?"

"No, all of the princesses. He's cancelled the feast as

well. I don't know why, but I have my suspicions and they're not good."

This wasn't about my magic then. I drew in a long breath and nodded. "I'm almost ready."

My maid did one last check of my gown and hair, and then I thanked her and quickly followed my aunt. Why would Father cancel the feast and summon all of us to his throne room? Was there a problem? Had he come to an agreement with the wizard king? My pulse quickened at the thought of seeing the dark man again. There was something about him that intrigued me, even though I'd probably never see him again after today.

"Have you met King Raith before?" I asked Dahlia, as we left the wing that held the royal quarters and approached the throne room. The castle had calmed considerably since I'd first returned, but there was still a tense feeling in the air, as if everyone was standing a little straighter and prepared for anything.

"Once, when he was only a child. Even then he was a dour thing. I can't imagine he's gotten much better with age. Not after his wife was murdered."

"She was murdered?" I knew Raith's wife had been killed before he became king, but nothing more. I'd never been good at keeping up with politics though. That was Lily's job and I'd been glad to leave her to it for my entire life. Now I wished I'd paid more attention in my lessons about the other kingdoms instead of spending all my time sneaking off to teach myself magic or daydreaming about being anywhere but in this frigid castle.

"So I've heard," Dahlia said. "I don't know much more than that."

I doubted that. Princess Dahlia was known as the Queen of Secrets for a reason, though she was not actually a queen in title. With her husband, Garon, she ran the Ravens, the King's network of spies, assassins, and thieves, and tended to know more than she should about just about everything and everyone, even if she didn't always deign to share.

"Did King Raith murder her?" I asked.

"No, of course not," Dahlia said. "Don't believe all those ridiculous stories about him. But don't underestimate him either. He's a formidable foe."

"I won't."

We approached the throne room and the guards opened the huge double doors for us. My other sisters were already inside, lined up in a row with a space for me between Lily and Jasmine. Dahlia gave my arm a quick squeeze before moving to her position behind the King's shoulder, appropriate for her role as both his sister and the royal advisor. Father sat on his throne glaring daggers at King Raith, who stood off to the side with his hands behind his back, a dark silhouette against the white stones behind him.

As I crossed the room, Raith's gaze met mine and my heartbeat quickened. He took a slow perusal of my entire body, his eyes lingering a touch longer on the bodice of my gown and the places where it hugged my curves. Oh yes, the red dress had definitely caught his attention.

"You're late, Rose," Father snapped.

"My apologies, your majesty," I said, as I hurried along. Even if I hadn't been last to arrive, he would have found something else to pick on, such as my hair or clothing. For him that was pretty minor criticism. He must be in a good mood tonight.

He flicked his fingers dismissively as I took my place in line as the second oldest daughter. Lily gave me a quick nod, while Jasmine flashed me a kind smile.

"Now that you're all here we can begin," Father said. "King Raith and I have come to an agreement that will end the war between our kingdoms, sealed with an alliance through marriage. As such, I've told him he may choose any one of you as his bride."

His *bride?* My sisters and I all glanced at each other as shock rippled through us. Jasmine's eyes were wide and Lily looked both stoic and worried. Down the line, Camellia's mouth hung open, Violet's brows were furrowed and thoughtful, and Iris had an impish grin on her face. I wasn't sure what my face showed in return. Even though the news was surprising, my shock was laced with relief that this long, drawn-out war would finally be over.

Father sat back on his throne and gestured toward us. "There you have it, Raith. My lovely daughters. I'm certain one of them will be suitable."

Raith's lips pressed into a tight line as he surveyed the six of us like we were horses he meant to purchase. Surely he wouldn't choose one of us based on looks alone? And did any of us have a say in the matter? It was just like our father to do something like this without asking any of us what *we* wanted. We were nothing but pawns to him.

Raith moved in front of Iris, towering above her in his black finery, and asked, "How old are you?"

"Twelve," she said, puffing up her chest proudly.

Raith arched a dark eyebrow at my father. "You would let me take this child as my bride?"

Father casually shrugged. "Some men like their women young."

My fists tightened, my nails digging into my skin, but I was comforted when Raith shook his head, his mouth twisted in disgust. He wouldn't choose Iris then, praise the Sun and Moon.

But none of my other sisters were safe.

As he stood in front of the twins, Camellia and Violet, my stomach turned. They were both only fifteen and would make terrible brides for him anyway. Camellia spent all her time practicing her combat skills with the other guards and almost always had a blade in her hand. Violet was happiest when she could devote an entire day to reading, and practically lived in the library. Neither one of them wished to be queen of anything, let alone Ilidan.

Raith turned to Jasmine next, who was seventeen years of age and possessed a wild beauty befitting a girl who loved the outdoors. She was the kindest and sweetest of us all, and I hated the idea of her marrying this dark, brooding man and becoming his queen. It would destroy her spirit.

His eyes skipped over me entirely, like he had no interest in me whatsoever. I supposed not after our awkward encounter earlier, but it still annoyed me. Was I not good enough to even be considered as his future bride?

Then of course there was Lily, who was meant to be the future queen of Talador. He couldn't choose her—I'd be surprised if our father even allowed it, since that would make *me* the heir. Besides, Lily had spent her entire life preparing to take the throne one day and would make an excellent ruler. Sending her to another kingdom would be devastating for all of us.

With each second Raith stood before Lily my terror grew, but then he shook his head. As he stepped back and swept his gaze over us, he asked, "Any volunteers?" The room remained silent and he clasped his hands behind his back, cutting a sharp profile. "No? Very well then. Perhaps we won't be able to come to an agreement after all. Perhaps I'll simply take your king's head in exchange for peace between our lands."

"That wasn't part of our bargain," Father growled.

"Silence," Raith called out. The guards touched their swords, but he cast them a stony look and they all froze. "I've amended our deal, and I'm beginning to think this might be the best solution for all of us. Surely none of your daughters wishes to be bound to me either."

Our king was cruel, cold, and had brought our kingdom to near ruin, but if I didn't act soon, one of my other sisters would volunteer to save him, simply because he was our father. I cared little for him, but I loved my sisters more than anything else in the world. I would do anything to protect them. *Anything.*

There was only one solution.

I stepped forward, facing Raith while my voice rang out through the throne room. "I volunteer to be your wife."

"You?" Father let out a harsh laugh. "I suppose you'll do anything to be queen, won't you?"

"Yes, that's it," I said, my voice dry. At his side, Dahlia gave me a quick nod, her eyes proud. She knew why I did this, even if he didn't.

Raith regarded me at last. "You are certain?"

All of my sisters looked positively shocked. I could tell Lily wanted to step in and save me, but I shook my head subtly at her. She bit her lip, her eyes pained, but she had to know this was the only option. I was the second daughter and had always known my role was to be married off in a way that benefited my kingdom. Becoming Raith's wife would bring much-needed peace to our people. If I could save my sisters at the same time, even better.

I gathered my strength and stood a little taller. "I'm certain."

"Will she do?" Father asked. "You're welcome to choose another if she's not to your liking. Rose is rather...headstrong."

I stared at Raith with a challenge in my eyes, silently daring him to even try choosing another. When he returned my defiant gaze, the faintest hint of a smile slowly touched his lips. It somehow made him even more handsome, and my heart skipped a beat at the sight.

"She'll do," he said, and relief lessened the weight on my shoulders.

"Fabulous," our king said. "We'll begin wedding preparations in the morning with the celebration to commence in a week's time—"

"Tomorrow," Raith said.

Father blinked, not used to being interrupted. "Excuse me?"

"We'll be married tomorrow, and we'll leave immediately after the wedding feast." The wizard king's voice left no room for argument. While Father sputtered, Raith turned to me and said, "Prepare your things. You have one night left in this castle."

I swallowed as the implications of what I'd done hit me. I'd agreed to marry this stranger and leave my home behind along with my sisters and my entire life, saying goodbye to everything I'd ever known and loved.

In one night, I'd no longer be a princess of Talador, but the queen of Ilidan.

FOUR

ROSE

We were dismissed from the throne room so that the two kings could discuss the details of their alliance further.

As soon as the doors shut, Lily grabbed my arm and dragged me into a chamber off to the side, while our other sisters followed at our heels. "Rose, what have you done?" she asked.

"What I had to do." I turned toward the rest of them. "We all know it had to be me."

Jasmine took my hand in hers. "I'd be happy to take your place. You don't need to do this."

Her face was so kind, and it broke my heart knowing I wouldn't see it every day anymore. I gave her hand a squeeze. "Yes, I do."

"Maybe he'll teach you magic," Iris piped up.

I smiled at her youthful exuberance, which I was truly going to miss. "Perhaps he will."

"He is rather handsome," Violet said, though her tone was entirely practical. "You could certainly do worse, as political marriages go. Your children will be attractive, at least."

Children? I hadn't considered them when I'd struck this bargain. Or that Raith and I would soon be consummating our marriage. The thought sent a rush of heat through me, not entirely unwanted.

"Not to mention, you'll be queen of one of the Six Kingdoms," Camellia said, and I noticed a sword hidden on her back under her dress. "You'll have King Raith's ear, and Ilidan's entire army at your command."

"Assuming my future husband listens to me at all," I said. "He seems rather...unchangeable."

"You're the most stubborn girl I know," Lily said, with a proud smile. "You'll make sure to get your way."

I laughed. "You may be right about that."

"Besides, it's a good sign he wants to end the war," she continued, her smile dropping. "Our people can't last much longer. Especially with the threat from Mesner rising."

"Enough of that," Dahlia said, as she stepped from the shadows. "We have a wedding to plan in only a few hours and we're all going to have to work together to make sure it's a celebration to remember. Jasmine, you're on flowers and decorations. Camellia, you'll oversee the guards and security for the event. Violet, research wedding traditions in Ilidan and help organize the ceremony. Iris, you're in charge of food for the wedding feast. And Lily and Rose, you're with me." She glanced between the six of us and clapped her hands. "Let's get to work."

The others rushed off to attend to their tasks, which were each perfect for their personalities. When they were out of earshot, Dahlia turned to me with an enigmatic smile. "Now then. There's something I need to give you. Lily should see it as well."

"What is it?" I asked.

"Follow me."

She led us through the cold stone halls of the castle, deep into an underground passage that smelled of mold and flickered with fading torchlight. I wasn't sure where we were going until Dahlia stopped to touch a random spot on the wall, which opened a secret tunnel with a groan of stone and steel. It seemed she knew of places in the castle that even the King didn't.

"What is this room?" Lily asked, as we followed our aunt inside, ducking to avoid hitting our heads on the low entrance.

Dahlia took us through the cramped tunnel, then produced a key and unlocked an old wooden door at the end. "A place where I keep things I don't want anyone else to find."

The door creaked open and we stepped into a hidden room full of treasures. Dusty chests, weathered books, and other assorted objects filled the small space and looked as though they hadn't been disturbed in some time. I spotted an old sword inlaid with a star ruby, a bow etched with silver runes, and a small cobweb-covered box that faintly glowed.

"This is where I kept your mother's spellbook all those years, so your father would never find it," Dahlia said, as she moved toward a large bronze chest in the corner. "Fellina instructed me to give it to you when you turned fifteen. But that wasn't all she left you."

"I don't understand," I said, as I glanced around the strange room. "Why would she do that?"

Dahlia opened the chest with a loud creak. "Fellina was a powerful wizard, as you know, but one thing that is rarely spoken of anymore is that she had an affinity for fortune runes."

"Fortune runes," Lily said, at my side. "As in, magic that predicts the future?"

"Indeed. Your mother saw her fate long before it came to pass, as well as both of yours." Dahlia got a distant look in her eyes, but then shook it off. "She saw mine as well."

"If that's true, then she knew..." My voice trailed off as emotion filled my chest.

She rested a hand on my shoulder. "Yes. She knew she would die giving birth to you."

"Why didn't she do anything to stop it? Or prevent it?" I'd lived my entire life with the guilt of killing my mother and the sadness over never knowing her, along with the hatred in my father's eyes whenever he looked at me. He blamed me for her death, and the absence of her presence had always weighed heavily on my shoulders. If she'd known it would happen, wouldn't she want to spare me from that, and from growing up without a mother?

"She didn't want to risk altering your future," Dahlia said. "Believe me, I pleaded with her for months. Fellina was my best friend and I begged her to change her fate when she told me she was going to die in childbirth. But she refused, and in her last breath she was content. She considered it her greatest honor to give birth to two smart, capable daughters she'd seen would both become queens one day. And she told me it was my duty to raise you and your sisters as best I could."

Lily wiped at her eyes. "Father never told us any of this."

"No, of course not. After Fellina died, Balsam was bereft for months, and when he decided to marry again, he ordered everything of your mother's destroyed. I managed to save a few things and stored them here where he would never find them."

"It's a wonder he didn't have me killed as well," I muttered.

Dahlia's face softened. "He would never do that. Yes, you remind him of his loss, but you remind him of her love too. He does care for you, in his own way."

I wasn't sure of that, but perhaps by marrying King Raith and saving our kingdom from further bloodshed I would earn a tiny bit of his respect. That would have to be enough.

Dahlia reached into the chest and drew out a long, white gown of sparkling silk encrusted with diamonds. "One of the things I saved from his purge was your mother's wedding gown. She told me to give it to you, Rose. For your wedding day."

My throat tightened at the sight of the beautiful dress that had once been worn by our mother. "I can't accept that. It should be Lily's, not mine."

Dahlia shook her head. "She has something for Lily's wedding as well, when the time comes. Don't worry about that."

"It's meant to be yours," Lily said. "Besides, Father would never allow me to wear her dress."

"But he'll let me?" I asked.

"He won't have a choice," Dahlia said. "King Raith demanded the wedding be held tomorrow and we don't have a lot of other options." She raised the gown up to my body, then had me hold it there while she searched for something in the room. "You're about the same size she was, so I know this will fit perfectly."

She drew a long sheet of fabric off a tall mirror, sending dust across the room and making us all cough. I caught sight of my reflection as I held the gown up to myself, and tears filled my eyes.

"It's perfect," Lily said, pressing a hand to her chest.

I nodded, unable to speak with all the emotions coursing through me. I'd thought the spellbook the only thing left of my mother's, but now I would be wearing her gown at my own wedding. Not only that, she'd purposefully left it for me, knowing we'd be in this situation. As I held the gown to my chest, I felt closer to her than ever before, and more confident in my decision to marry Raith. If Mother had wanted this future for me, it must not be too bad. What else had she seen?

"You look just like Fellina." Dahlia gathered me in a hug, wrapping me in her warm arms. "You girls are the daughters that Garon and I could never have. I love you all like my own children, and I'm so proud of you. I know your mother would be too."

My throat tightened as I clung to her. She was the closest thing we'd all had to a mother too. "Thank you. For everything."

When she let me go, Lily immediately grabbed me in a tight hug of her own. "It should be me marrying that horrible man," she said, her voice breaking. "I'm supposed to be the one protecting you."

"We both know it had to be me. You have to stay here and become queen, and the others have their own paths to follow. I've always known I'd be married off to suit Father's needs, although I never expected it to be to King Raith, of all people." I pulled back just enough to give Lily a brave smile. My older sister by only one year, but sometimes it felt like ten. She'd always taken care of me, but now it was my turn. "Besides, I've long dreamed of exploring new lands. Now I'll get my chance."

Lily's eyes were wet with unshed tears. "I can't imagine my life without you. I don't want you to leave."

I didn't want to leave either, despite my words. Even if I'd always known this day would come, the thought of leaving behind my family and my home was hard to accept.

Especially since I'd be going to live in a kingdom that had long been our enemy, with a strange, brooding man as my husband. But I would agree to it again, a hundred times over, if it meant protecting my kingdom and my family.

I took Lily's hands and squeezed them. "Soon we'll both be queens of one of the Six Kingdoms, and we'll be able to bring lasting peace to our lands. Together we will change the entire world for the better. Just like our mother would have wanted."

I turned back to the mirror and gazed at my reflection, noting the fear in my eyes despite my bold words. There were so many unknowns—what marriage to Raith would be like, how I would fare in his kingdom, whether his people would even accept me—but I would face those challenges as they came. I only prayed to the Sun and Moon I could live up to my mother's dreams and be the queen she'd hoped I would become.

FIVE

RAITH

The wedding lasted an eternity. Or that's how it felt, anyway.

As the sun neared the horizon and night threatened to take over the world, Princess Rose and I stood in the open-air temple of the Sun and Moon before a priest who wore the traditional robes of gold and silver. As he raised his hands to the sky and recited his blessing, Rose faced me wearing a sparkling white dress that clung to her curves and contrasted with her dark beauty to only make her more stunning. Yet every time I looked at her, I saw Silena on our wedding day instead and the old, familiar pain gripped my heart. After three years I thought I'd be over the ache of losing my wife, but it seemed I would never fully recover from it. This wedding at sunset only brought back those once-fond memories and reminded me of how much I had lost.

I avoided looking at Rose by studying the rest of the people gathered among us. King Balsam watched the ceremony with a bored expression, as if he didn't care at all that I was taking his daughter away. His sister's face was stoic, though she tightly clutched the hand of her husband, a tall man with dark eyes that seemed to hold many secrets. The eldest daughter, Princess Lily, stood beside them with her hands clasped in front of her, wearing a tiara made to look like ice shards. I'd nearly chosen her for my bride just to spite her father, since it was well known she was his favorite. I'd also considered choosing Princess Jasmine, who wore a yellow gown that seemed to match her cheerful disposition. The others were far too young, both those blond twins and the red-haired child, so I'd dismissed them immediately. But in the end, Rose had been the only one bold enough to volunteer, as I'd known she would. Just as I'd known from the moment I first looked into her amber eyes that I could choose no other, no matter how hard I'd tried to deny it. She was the only one strong enough to be Queen of Ilidan, even if something told me she would be trouble.

As the sun vanished and the moon rose in the sky, the ceremony concluded with the customary exchanging of ancestral rings. Silena's wedding ring had once been my grandmother's, but now hung from a chain around my neck, tucked inside my black shirt along with the wedding ring she had given me. This morning I'd removed it from my hand for the first time in four years in preparation for a new ring to replace it tonight.

I slid a ruby-encrusted band onto Rose's fingers. "I gift to you the ring of my mother, Queen Casnia of Ilidan, as a symbol of our marriage."

Rose admired the ring on her hand as snow began to fall from the night sky. I mentally cast a rune to shield her from it, along with the increasingly frigid wind around us. In that thin silk gown she had little protection from the harsh weather of this land. Her eyes raised to watch the snow fall in a wide circle around her. When she realized what I'd done she smiled at me, and at that moment I saw only her.

Our eyes locked and something like a spark passed between us. My throat tightened, my chest clenched, and I looked away quickly. *No.* I would not feel anything for my new bride. I had nothing left in my heart but darkness and pain. Rose's beauty and strength would not change that.

She took my hand and placed the ring on my finger, drawing my attention again. "I gift to you the ring of my great-grandfather, King Rowan of Talador, as a symbol of our marriage."

The ring was made of polished silver inlaid with sapphires and was a bit loose, but it was likely the best they could do on such short notice. Once both bands were on our fingers we were instructed to clasp hands while the priest finished his ceremony. Sparks flared as we touched, but I did my best to ignore them. Rose gazed into my eyes and I stared at her chin, willing this moment to end already.

The priest raised his hands again to the sky. "Blessed by the Sun and Moon, witnessed by the Stars, I hereby pronounce your union sacred and binding. May the Celestials watch over you both for all your days."

"Finally," I muttered, as I yanked my hands away from Rose. Her face fell, and I immediately wished I'd never said a thing.

No, it had to be this way. The sooner she realized this would never be a love-filled marriage, the better. She would be Queen of Ilidan and would have to find purpose in that, because there would be nothing between us except this political alliance we'd both been forced into.

Although there was still the magic problem. Even now I saw Rose eyeing the snow falling away from her and knew her clever mind was working. Her gift was strong, but untrained and clumsy. She'd likely found one old spellbook in a dusty corner of the castle and taught herself how to cast a few runes, but she would only injure herself—or someone else—if she kept that up. She had to be properly trained. By me, unfortunately, since there was no one else to do it.

Princess Lily also had the gift, but it wasn't nearly as strong. Merely a flicker that could have been built into a flame if nurtured, but that seemed unlikely now, especially with her father's hatred of wizards. The young one, Iris, had the gift as well, and I suspected she would be powerful once she came into her magic in the next year or two.

Neither one of them was my problem. Rose, on the other hand, was. I'd need to begin her training soon, even if I was reluctant to spend much time with her. But magic might protect her from the growing darkness inside Ilidan, though I would try to shield her from it as much as possible. And now that I'd ended the war with Talador, I could focus on the bigger threat—and find a way to save my kingdom.

SIX

ROSE

After the ceremony ended, we all retired to the great hall for the wedding feast. Father stood at the head of the room and recited a bland speech about how Talador and Ilidan were putting the past behind them and becoming allies for the first time in many generations. I tried to listen, but kept glancing at the ring on my hand, admiring the rubies while wondering how I'd ended up both a wife and a queen on this whirlwind of a day.

I knew little of Ilidan, yet in a few hours it would be my new home. I'd never gone farther than a few miles from Winton Castle, but soon I'd be journeying to a different kingdom. A mixture of apprehension and excitement fought for dominance inside me at the thought. For years I'd dreamed of something more than this life in a dreary castle, yet now I wasn't sure I was ready for it.

After Father finished his speech and the audience

cheered for our union, the wedding feast commenced. Everyone I'd ever known sat at the long wooden tables and began to eat, while soft music played behind us. Raith was seated to my left, his perfectly sculpted face impassive and cold, his formal black clothes a sharp contrast to my bright white gown. He'd barely said a word to me all day and acted as if he'd rather be anywhere but at my side, even though he was the one who'd agreed to this marriage with my father. I knew it was a political alliance, and one he'd been coerced into, but surely he must hope for something more from it as well?

"Is the celebration not to your liking?" I asked him, keeping my voice low so only he could hear me amid the loud chatter in the room.

"It's fine." He stabbed at his food with his fork as if it had personally offended him.

"Then perhaps I'm the one not to your liking?" I asked before I could think better of it. "Maybe you would have preferred one of my other sisters?" His face remained impassive, and I huffed softly when he didn't answer. "Well, too bad. I'm your wife now and you'll have to deal with it. Just like I'll have to deal with your brooding self for the rest of my days."

His storm gray eyes found mine, and he looked almost amused at my outburst. "My brooding self simply dislikes weddings and being away from my home. That is all."

"Oh." I dropped my gaze to my plate and took a long sip of mead to cover my embarrassment. "What can you tell me of Ilidan?"

"It's warmer than Talador," he said, his tone dry.

I snorted. "Everywhere is warmer than here, or so I'm told."

I waited for him to go on, but that seemed to be the extent of our discussion. We wouldn't have much conversation in our marriage, it seemed. What *did* he expect of me anyway? A woman who would bear his heirs and stay out of his way? If so, he was going to be sorely disappointed.

"Ilidan is known for having dense forests, rich farmlands, and fine woolen textiles," Lily said from across the table, where she'd obviously been eavesdropping. She'd never been to Ilidan herself either, so she was simply reciting what she'd learned from her tutors. Tutors I should have listened to more, instead of having my head in the clouds all the time. In my defense, no one ever predicted I'd marry the King of Ilidan, of all men. His people had been our enemies for so long, we only spoke of them in terms of strategy and war. Not marriage.

Raith's dark gaze turned to Lily next. "We're also one of the top exporters of iron and slate, but I doubt Rose cares about that."

I sat up straighter. "You're wrong. I want to learn everything I can about my new home. Especially if I'm to help you rule it."

His scowl only deepened at that, while Lily watched us with wary eyes but had nothing further to offer. I was on my own, and would have to learn about Ilidan while I was there. No matter. I'd study what I could, ask questions of everyone who would listen, and do whatever it took to be a good queen, even if only to preserve the peace between the two kingdoms. I might not have planned for this role, but I was going to do my best at it.

As the meal finished, the music picked up and people began pairing off and moving to the far end of the hall to begin dancing. Many of my sisters joined in—Camellia with one of the guards, Jasmine with another nobleman, and Iris with a boy her age—and I ached to join them. To twirl around in my skirts, lose myself in the music, and have one last night of freedom and youth.

One glance at my new husband's serious face put that out of my mind. "I'm guessing you're not fond of dancing," I said.

"Not particularly."

I sighed and smoothed the skirt of my dress. "Why am I not surprised?"

Raith suddenly rose to his feet and my hopes lifted, thinking he'd changed his mind, especially when he offered his hand to help me up. As my fingers slid into his and he pulled me toward him, an awareness crept over me like a spark being lit. In his formal black suit, he looked especially handsome, and when our eyes locked, my breath hitched. His gaze held so many secrets and so much knowledge I wanted to uncover—about Ilidan, about my new husband, and about the magic that came so easily to him. And other knowledge too, of carnal pleasures I dared not think about for fear he'd see the flush of heat in my cheeks.

But my hopes of dancing were dashed when he said, "If the feast is over, then it's time to say our goodbyes."

"Already?" My throat tightened at the thought of all I was leaving behind. My bags were packed and I'd already made peace with my new life, but now that it was time to go, a mixture of sadness and fear gripped my heart. Yet there was something else fluttering about in my chest too—excitement. I was finally leaving this cold, dreary castle behind and journeying somewhere new, where I might be more than second daughter and spare to the heir. In Ilidan, of all places, I might find my true purpose.

Raith turned toward my father, his hand still clutching mine. "King Balsam, thank you for the hospitality and the alliance. I'm sure you're quite ready for me to be gone from your kingdom."

Father chuckled softly. "Impatient to be alone with your bride? I know how that is." He waved his hand. "Go then and have my blessings. I'll hold to the terms of our agreement."

"As will I." Raith bowed his head, before turning toward me. "I hope you've said your goodbyes already."

My eyes widened and I was able to cast one quick glance at Lily, her face full of sorrow and love, before the shadows crept over me and the noise of the feast faded away. I gasped as the world around me went dark and silent, my skin tingling with the feel of magic. My fingers tightened around Raith's, his stiff presence at my side the only sign I wasn't alone in the black ink that had swallowed everything around us.

The darkness slowly receded. Dim light returned, and with it, the sound of flames flickering in a draft. I drew a deep breath as I took in my new surroundings. Gone was the great hall of Talador's royal palace, and in its place was a small, empty room carved from smooth black stone and lit with dozens of candles. We must have teleported, though I hadn't seen Raith cast a rune.

"Where are we?" I asked.

Raith dropped my hand like it was a dead fish he couldn't wait to be rid of. "Your new home."

SEVEN

ROSE

I spun around to face the infuriating wizard. "You could have given me a chance to say goodbye!"

Raith threw open the door and strode from the room. "You had all day to do that."

I huffed and chased after him down a hallway of the same black stone, made glaringly bright with torches every few feet. "Some warning would have been nice."

"I told you we would leave as soon as the wedding feast was over."

"Yes, and that still gave me a few more hours!"

An older, stately gentleman emerged from a doorway. "Good, you've returned. The ledgers you requested are in your study and—" He cut off when he saw me, taking in the sight of my diamond-covered wedding gown and silver tiara with surprise.

"Rose, this is Oren," Raith said. "He runs the castle and acts as my advisor in most matters."

"Your majesty, it is an honor to welcome you to Ilidan," Oren said, with a deep bow. It took me a moment to realize he was addressing *me* as "majesty." Another thing I would have to get used to now that I was a queen.

"It's a pleasure to meet you," I said, mustering the best smile I could. I studied Oren's lined face for any sign of disgust or reluctance, but he was either too well-trained for that or truly had none, even though only hours earlier our kingdoms had been at war. Even if Oren didn't dislike me on sight, I couldn't expect others to treat me so well. What would the people of Ilidan think once they discovered they had a new, unexpected queen, who had formerly been their enemy?

"I've already prepared the royal consort's chambers and had your belongings moved into them. Please let me know if there is anything else you require."

"Oh," I said. "Thank you. I hadn't realized my things were already here."

"I brought them over earlier," Raith said.

I was torn between feeling impressed with his teleportation magic and resigned that even my belongings had been brought here without my knowledge. Everything was happening so quickly, and it felt like control of my life was slipping out of my grasp completely. Not that I'd ever had much control, but I'd cherished what little I could chip away from my father's rule. Now even that was gone.

We moved through what I now realized was Ilidan's

main residence for the royal family, Varlock Castle. From the stories I'd heard I'd gotten the impression it was a gothic, foreboding keep full of cobwebs, dark magic, and darker secrets. A place where if you opened a closet door, you might find a dead body stashed inside. I didn't see any cobwebs, but I couldn't rule out the rest just yet.

We stepped into a large entry decorated with hundreds of candles, torches, and braziers scattered around the room. They illuminated every corner and nook, making the space almost as bright as if it were the middle of the day. Perhaps to lighten up the otherwise dreary castle, which seemed to be made entirely of that smooth black stone that danced with the reflections of flame and light. The castle was disturbingly quiet, and only four guards in red and black armor stood around the room despite its size. Then again, Raith had entered my kingdom unprotected—maybe he believed his magic kept the castle safe. I was certainly familiar with the arrogance of kings, though my father preferred to show his power by filling our castle with as many soldiers as possible.

"Your rooms are this way, your majesty," Oren said. "If you'll follow me..."

I hesitated, glancing back at Raith before addressing Oren. "Would you please give us a moment?"

"Of course," Oren said, before stepping away to a discreet distance.

"What now?" I asked Raith quietly, hoping he understood the silent questions hiding between those two words.

Where do we go from here as husband and wife? What is my role as queen? What do you expect of me?

"I have some business to attend to in my study," Raith said, his voice clipped. "Oren will show you to your chambers and we'll discuss everything else tomorrow."

I smoothed the skirt of my wedding dress, my hands restless. "Will you join me tonight?"

He frowned, but his eyes followed my hands before sliding slowly back up my body to my face. "You must be exhausted."

"I'm fine."

He turned away with a sharp exhale. "Go to your rooms. I'll meet with you later."

Later. A trickle of warmth spread through me at this small victory and at the anticipation of our future encounter. I inclined my head slightly. "I'll see you then."

But as I turned away, he stopped me with one word. "Wait."

My pulse raced as I faced him again. "Yes?"

"There's one more thing," he said, his voice turning dark and commanding. "You are to never leave the castle alone, and must never step foot outside at night. Do you understand?"

I blinked at him. "Why?"

"It's not safe for you." He took a step forward, until he towered over me. "Promise me you'll stay inside after sundown."

I opened my mouth to protest, but held my tongue at the last moment. Raith must be worried I was in danger from people in Ilidan who might want to punish me for every-thing my kingdom had done. There would be many who couldn't believe we were at peace now, or wouldn't want to accept it. Was that why there were so few guards? Had he removed any that he didn't feel could be trusted completely?

"I'll stay inside," I said. "Until it's safe."

He gave me a hard stare that never seemed to end, before he finally turned on his heel and walked away without another word. I watched him disappear, the door banging shut behind him, and sighed. So much for my grand wedding night.

Oren led me down more overly illuminated corridors, and our footsteps were the only sounds echoing throughout the eerily empty castle. The few servants we did see dropped to a hasty bow, then spoke in hushed whispers as soon as we'd passed them by. The guards ignored us completely, their eyes watching the shadows while their armor gleamed under the firelight.

"You certainly keep this place aglow," I said to Oren as we climbed a stone staircase and turned down another bright hallway.

He nodded solemnly. "To keep the shadows away,."

"Of course," I said, as if I knew what he meant, though I wasn't sure why that was so important. Perhaps it was a normal custom in Ilidan? Further proof I had a lot to learn about my new home. If only I'd had more time before the wedding and our departure, I could have studied up on Ilidan instead of arriving in my new home feeling lost and ignorant. Something I would have to rectify tomorrow.

Oren nodded to a heavy door as we passed by it. "This is the monarch's chambers, though King Raith spends little time inside them. He can usually be found in his study."

He continued to the next door and opened it with a key. We entered a sitting room decorated in dark red and black brocade, with tall arched ceilings and huge windows on one side. The hearth was going strong to combat the night's chill, although compared to Talador it was quite warm here. No shadows touched the room thanks to the candles covering nearly every surface. Like the rest of Varlock Castle, someone had gone to a lot of trouble making sure this room was brightly lit.

"These are the royal consort's chambers," Oren said as we stepped inside. "They haven't been used in some time, not since the King's father passed about six years ago, but we have aired them out and prepared them for your arrival as best we could on such short notice."

"I appreciate that. This has happened rather quickly for all of us."

"Indeed. King Raith only informed us of your marriage this afternoon when he brought over some of your belongings. It was certainly a...surprise."

"For Raith and I as well," I said, with a wry smile.

He gestured to the room. "As royal consort, you have your own personal sitting room, washroom, and bedroom. I'm sure you'll want to update them to your own style, of course."

"Did Raith's wife not stay here?"

He stiffened up, his face going blank. "Lady Silena

passed before he became king. They lived in another part of the castle." He moved to the door and bowed again. "Please let me know if there is anything else you need."

"Thank you, Oren." He seemed hesitant to speak at all about the lost princess, which I supposed was understandable, especially if she was well-loved. But I doubted Raith would tell me anything about her, so I had to get information wherever I could.

As soon as he left, a girl about my age entered and dropped into a deep curtsy. She wore a plain blue dress and had blond hair tied back tightly. "Your majesty, I am Loura and it is a great honor to serve you as your lady's maid."

"It's nice to meet you, Loura. Please, call me Rose." I hadn't been allowed a single lady's maid to accompany me to Ilidan, which still stung. But no matter. Though I was completely cut off from my home, I would do what I could to form new bonds here.

"Yes, Queen Rose," she said, her cheeks flushed.

I gave her a kind smile. "Just Rose is fine. I'm still getting used to the new title, and it's all a bit overwhelming."

Loura looked worried at the suggestion she could speak to me without formality, but nodded. "Of course, your..." She swallowed back the word and nodded again.

After taking another look at the sitting room, I moved into the bedroom. It was decorated similarly, with a large canopied bed and an ornate wooden wardrobe, along with a locked door on one side.

"Where does this go?" I asked, flicking open the lock.

"That connects to the King's chambers," Loura said.

"Ahh," I said, with heat rising to my cheeks at the thought of Raith walking through the door later tonight. I left it unlocked. "I suppose I should get ready for him."

Loura moved to the wardrobe. "I hope you don't mind, but I've already put away all your things. I can order up a bath for you as well, if you'd like."

"That would be lovely, thank you."

After she left the room, I found myself alone for the first time that day. I took a long, deep breath as I sat on the edge of my new bed. In my new room. In my new home. In my new role as wife and queen.

Emotion clouded my eyes and choked my throat at the thought of everything I'd left behind and everything I still had to learn. All I wanted to do was collapse on the bed, wrap my arms around myself, and sob, but I forcibly pushed those thoughts away. I would not cry, and I would not be upset. I'd volunteered for this life. I'd saved my sisters and my father. I'd brought peace to two kingdoms. Yes, there were many things I'd have to adjust to in my new life, but I could handle whatever challenges would come. On my own if I had to.

I glanced at the door connecting my bedroom to Raith's. Perhaps I wasn't entirely on my own. He'd been forced into this marriage too, and together we would have to make the best of this arrangement. Truly I was lucky to be married to a man I found attractive and not someone as old as my father. Hopefully Raith found me at least a little appealing as well.

Soon he would visit to consummate our marriage and

begin the process of creating an heir. I'd never been with a man before, although I'd shared a few torrid kisses and heavy touches in secret, but I wasn't afraid of what would happen. If anything, I was strangely excited. A delicious heat moved through me at the thought of Raith climbing into this giant bed and looking at me with those brooding gray eyes as he moved over my body. I pictured kissing that sharp jaw, tangling my fingers in his silky dark hair, and exploring what he kept hidden under all those severe black clothes.

My bath was brought up and Loura helped me prepare myself, making my hair smell of lavender and my skin smooth and clean. She left my dark brown locks long and flowing about my shoulders, and then I donned a chemise so thin my nipples could be seen through it. Once done, she left with a curtsy and a knowing gleam in her eye.

Then I waited. He'd said he would come to me later, but how late exactly did he mean? Surely he wouldn't take too long?

I lounged on the bed, trying to imagine what pose I should use when he entered. I was no seductress, but I wanted him to desire me. I got the feeling he did, from the fleeting looks he'd given me before, but I was no expert...and Raith was harder to read than most men anyway.

After a few minutes I got bored and began exploring my rooms. They contained little of interest, which I supposed made sense when they had been empty and unused for years. I did check that all my things had arrived safely, including my mother's spellbook, which Loura had left out on a desk in my sitting room. Here I wouldn't need to hide it, I realized with relief. I ran my fingers over the old leather, finding comfort in the familiar feel, before continuing my investigation.

A small bookcase held titles that sounded like a total bore to read, but I'd probably force myself through them since they were about Ilidan's economics, geography, and history. I peered through the windows and made out a large garden underneath the moonlight, which I hoped to explore tomorrow. Like the interior, the entire perimeter of the palace was illuminated with an abundance of torchlight, as if trying to fight off the night itself.

As I let the curtain fall, something large and dark moved outside on the edge of the garden, with what appeared to be wings. I looked again, scanning the grounds for whatever I'd seen from the corner of my eye, but it was gone. An animal, perhaps, though I couldn't imagine anything that size except perhaps a bear. Did they even have bears in Ilidan? Except bears didn't have wings. I peered through the curtain again and shook my head. There was nothing at all outside. I was merely tired and imagining things.

An hour passed and I checked the door to Raith's room, making sure my side was unlocked. A terrible curiosity over-came me, and I had the strongest desire to slip into his room and learn whatever I could about him, or perhaps wait for him in his own bed, but I restrained myself. He would no doubt be furious with me for encroaching on his private space that way.

Eventually I blew out a few of the candles and crawled

into bed to wait for him there, but my eyes grew heavy and soon I was curling up in the soft blankets. Exhaustion caught up to me after the long day and my hasty wedding, and I was sure he would forgive me if I took a little nap before his arrival.

I fell asleep immediately, and when I woke, the sun's light was already creeping through the drapes covering the windows. Only then did I realize what I should have always known—Raith wasn't coming.

EIGHT

RAITH

As dawn broke through the castle, and the torches and candles were extinguished with relief, I glanced through a handful of papers, reading the same thing on every one of them. Fear, death, and despair, and I was no closer to figuring out how to stop it. I dropped the missives on my desk and dragged a hand through my hair. Something had to be done and quickly. Now that Talador's army was no longer at our borders, I could shift my focus and my resources to this problem to solve it soon—or my kingdom would be lost.

"Another report from Levanston," Oren said, from his place in front of my desk. "The shadows have taken over two more houses there, and the dark beasts roam the streets at night."

"I'll visit the town tonight and see what I can do," I said, my voice weary. I'd already been there a week ago and fought back the darkness, but it always returned, stronger than ever. "And the Shadow Lord?"

"No sightings in the last three days, as far as I know."

I pinched the bridge of my nose, trying to ease the ache in my forehead. "He will be back soon, no doubt. We must be ready."

"Of course." He gave me a once-over heavy with scrutiny. "Did you sleep at all last night?"

"I got a few hours." I thought I did, anyway. I'd spent the night catching up on ledgers I'd missed while I was in Talador, then passed out on my chaise lounge once my eyes became too heavy. I remembered little else, other than the same frustration I felt every night as I tried and failed to find a solution to our problem, along with the new mix of desire and apprehension at the thought of my bride upstairs.

"I suspect you weren't awake all night for the reason you should have been," Oren said.

"What's that supposed to mean?"

"You know exactly what I speak of." He held my gaze. "Your new wife is lovely, isn't she?"

"I barely noticed," I lied.

Oren let out a soft snort. He was the only one who could get away with such insolence, but I appreciated his honesty and that he talked to me like a friend and not a king. He'd been my mother's advisor as well due to his shrewd thinking and unfailing loyalty. "I heard she waited up all night for you to join her in her room, but you never did."

"Is that what your judgmental look has been about this morning?" I asked, moving out from behind my desk to stare through the window at the palace's garden. "I have no intention of visiting her room anytime soon, not that it's any of your business."

"The royal line is my business, and you need an heir. I know you're still mourning Princess Silena, but—"

I spun around to face him. "Do not speak her name to me!"

Oren released a long, disappointed sigh. "Apologies, my lord. Nevertheless, your marriage requires consummation, and your royal line must continue. If something should happen to you, especially with the way you're risking your neck in such foolish ways these days, your kingdom will go to your cousin, Lord Malren."

"Don't remind me." Malren was the worst type of man, one who cared little for others and only for himself. He was a disgrace to my family's legacy and would lead this kingdom to ruin. I would never let that happen.

"Then find a way to make it work with your new queen, and quickly. Close your eyes and think of someone else if you must, but get it done—for your kingdom's sake."

Closing my eyes and thinking of someone else wasn't an option, not with Rose. The problem was that I wanted her too much already, and that path led to things I couldn't deal with right now. Or ever.

I turned toward Oren and used my most commanding tone, which never worked on him anyway. "I have other matters that are more pressing right now, but I will take your concerns under advisement and handle it as I see fit."

"Very well," he said, with a disapproving sniff. "Just

remember what your mother always told you. The most important thing in life is family. Even for a king."

Queen Casnia had been both a wise ruler and a great mother, and I'd believed those words for the longest time. Then my family was taken from me by the King of Talador, who was my new father-in-law in a cruel twist of fate. The thought of having a family again and putting the people I cared about at risk was unbearable, especially with the darkness spreading inside my kingdom. But Oren was right, and I'd have to find a way to make this situation with Rose agreeable or my kingdom would suffer for it. She was my wife and I couldn't avoid her forever.

An idea came to mind. "Call the Queen to my study."

A small, triumphant smile touched Oren's lips as he bowed. "As you wish."

I returned to my desk to finish my correspondence, until the lady herself walked into my study, alone. As my gaze rose to take her in, my breath left me in a rush. She wore a deep purple gown that was fairly plain, yet somehow only made her own beauty more striking. Her dark hair was piled atop her head in an intricate fashion, and I couldn't help but stare at the graceful slope of her neck and wonder how it would feel to place my lips there.

"Good morning, Raith," she said. There was a trace of annoyance in her voice and a challenge in her amber eyes, I assumed because I'd summoned her at such an early hour instead of letting her sleep in longer. Too bad. She'd have to get used to our schedule here—we didn't waste even a second of daylight.

She waited for me to speak, but as I gazed at her I forgot my original reason for calling her here. Sun and Moon, she was beautiful. That soft, creamy skin, those perfect red lips, and those lush, firm breasts... I cleared my throat and forced myself to focus. "Is everything in the castle to your liking?"

"Yes, it's quite lovely. I look forward to seeing more of it today."

"And you slept well, I hope?"

Her eyes narrowed the slightest bit. "I did."

"Good." I rose to my feet. "If you'll follow me, we'll begin your training."

"Training?" she asked. "What sort of training?"

"Your magical training, of course."

NINE

ROSE

My annoyance at Raith's absence last night faded away in an instant. I hurried after him as he left his study and headed down the corridor. "You plan to teach me magic?"

"I do. You have some raw talent for it, but you've clearly never had any real magical education. It would be irresponsible to leave you untrained." He stopped in front of a plain black door and removed a key from his coat pocket. "Have you had any sort of mentor before?"

"I'm self-taught," I said, standing up straighter. Even though I hadn't attended the fancy magic school in Korelan, I'd done the best I could with what I'd had.

"Somehow that doesn't surprise me."

With a click, his key unlocked the heavy door, and he slowly eased it open to reveal a dark, musty room with no windows. With a quick rune drawn in the air, he made a candelabra overhead flare to life. Bookshelves lined each wall with ancient, dusty tomes, and a long, wooden table stood in the center of the room, covered with vials, bottles, and flasks. As I gazed around I also spotted a human skull, a small dagger, and jars full of stones and crystals.

"What is this place?" I asked, as he locked the door behind us.

"This was once my father's magical workshop. Now it's passed to me."

"He was a wizard too?"

"Yes, born in Korelan. His sister is the current Archwizard, in fact."

Oh. I should have known that already. "How did he and your mother meet?"

He removed his long black coat and hung it on a small hook. "My mother was already Queen of Ilidan then, and even younger than I am now when she took the throne. She journeyed to Korelan on a diplomatic mission and met my father there. According to them, it was love at first sight. They were married a week later and were disgustingly in love their entire lives."

I smiled at his story. His parents' tale was so different from my father's many marriages that always ended in death or exile. "Perhaps hasty weddings are a family tradition."

He smirked and moved to the nearest bookshelf, where he began searching for a title. I surveyed the room, studying the strange liquids and powders stored on a nearby shelf, but no matter how much I wanted to explore every inch of the place I schooled myself to stillness and patience. It was hard and quite unlike me, but I was trying to show Raith I was ready to be the best magical student he'd ever had. All my life I'd dreamed of learning to use magic like my mother and now I had the chance—I wasn't about to waste it.

"Have you trained anyone before?" I asked.

"No. You will be my first and likely only apprentice." He pulled a book off the shelf. "It's a shame your father never sent you and Lily to Korelan for schooling. I suppose he won't send young Iris either, for that matter."

"He would have if not for his last wife. She soured him on magic and ruined everything for the rest of us." Iris's mother Riala had been caught having an affair, and when my father sent guards after her, she used magic to murder them all and escape. She'd been officially exiled, but no one knew where she'd gone or where she'd been hiding all this time, or if she was even still alive. After that, my father banned all magic from our kingdom. He'd always been suspicious of it, especially after magic couldn't save my mother, and Riala's betrayal was the final straw.

"So I've heard." Raith grabbed another two books and set them on top of the other, forming a growing pile in his arms.

Impatience and curiosity won out, and I inched closer to the table in the middle, eyeing what was on it. All the vials and bottles had runes etched into them, though I didn't recognize most of the symbols. "Did you attend the school in Korelan as well, or did your father teach you?"

"Both." He turned toward me and shoved the giant stack of books into my arms. "For your first lesson, read all of these and then write up a short summary of what you've learned about the history of magic and the original runemakers. Once that's done, we'll begin the next part of your training."

I staggered under the weight of the books and gaped at him. "You want me to read *all* of these?"

"Yes, ideally in the next week or two. Will that be a problem?"

I set the books down on the table, accidentally knocking into some empty vials. "No, but I'm not a complete beginner. I already know many spells and how to cast them. I was hoping you'd show me some new runes, like the one for teleportation, not give me long, stuffy texts about the history of magic."

"How can you expect to understand a thing if you don't know it's history? Besides, I've seen your poor excuse of a spell, and it would be easier for both of us if you *were* a beginner." He gave me a withering look and crossed to the other side of the room to grab another book. "Teleportation is a high level spell that very few can ever master. You have a long way to go before I'd even let you attempt it. And why would you even need such a spell? Do you hope to use it to escape this place?"

I planted my hands on my hips, my defenses prickling at his words. "My spells are not poor, I was simply startled by your sudden appearance the other day. And I have no intention of escaping, but it'd be nice to be able to visit my sisters whenever I wanted."

He added the new book to my already tall stack, likely just because I'd argued with him. "If you performed a teleportation rune wrong, you would be stuck in the Shadow Lands forever. No, you won't be learning that one anytime soon."

I sighed and flipped through the crinkling pages with words in tiny font that made my eyes cross. "Fine, but couldn't you simply give me a quick summary of these books so we could move on to the actual training? I'm much more of a hands-on learner."

"I could, but I will not. If you need a place to study other than your sitting room, there's a library on the first floor you're welcome to use." He turned his back to me and began inspecting one of the vials. "Let me know once you've finished and then we'll move on to the next lesson."

That was a dismissal if I'd ever heard one. Resigned to my fate, I grabbed my heavy stack of books and moved to the door, but hesitated in front of it. There was something else I wanted to know, and if I didn't ask now, I wasn't sure I'd have the courage to do so later.

I took a deep breath and faced Raith again. "Why didn't you come to my room last night?"

He jerked his head toward me. "Your room?"

Was he going to make me spell it out for him? "Yes. We are married, after all."

He examined another vial with his brow furrowed. "I had other matters to attend to last night."

"Of course." I paused. "Then you'll come tonight?"

"No."

"I see." I tried to keep the disappointment from my voice,

but it was difficult. Rejection always hurt, even from a man I barely knew. I swallowed and tried to smooth over the awkward moment. "I understand. We only just met, after all. We need some time to grow better accustomed to each other."

"No," he said again, more forcefully. "I have no plans to visit your room. Not tonight. Not tomorrow night. Not any time in the foreseeable future."

"You don't?" I blinked at him. "But...surely you need an heir."

"Eventually, yes. We'll face that problem later."

I blew out a long breath, unease swirling in my stomach. "Later."

His stormy eyes swept over my body like a caress. "Are you so eager for me to join you in bed?"

Heat rushed to my cheeks. "No! Definitely not."

He turned back to his vials and sounded almost bored when he asked, "What is it then?"

"I simply want to know my role here as your wife. What do you want from this marriage? An apprentice, fine. But what else? A friend? A partner?" My voice dropped to nearly a whisper. "A lover?"

His back stiffened, and when he spoke next, his tone was hard. "I don't expect anything from you. We were both forced into this marriage and we must try to make the best of it. If you're hoping for a grand romance, you will be sorely disappointed. Best to get that foolish notion out of your head now."

"Trust me, I don't," I snapped, as his words burned

through me. "You've made it quite clear you have zero interest in me in that regard."

I threw open the door and stormed out before he could cut me down more. Perhaps it *was* foolish to hope for a marriage filled with love, but didn't everyone wish for such a thing? Even a princess who knew her role was to be married in a political alliance could dream of romance, no matter how unlikely it was to come about. At the very least, I'd hoped Raith and I could be friends someday, but he wanted nothing more than a student, and didn't seem particularly excited about me playing *that* role either.

What had I expected, truly? He hadn't chosen me for his bride. He would have picked another if I hadn't volunteered. Perhaps the idea of lying with me completely disgusted him. Perhaps he looked at me and only remembered the wife who'd died, who no doubt would have made a better queen. Perhaps we would never be more than acquaintances forced to live together in the same castle.

I'd have to find my happiness and fulfillment in some other way, it seemed. Starting with this giant stack of books.

TEN

ROSE

I spent my entire day in the library reading through the dreadfully dull books Raith assigned me, until I thought I would fall asleep if I kept going. Oren also pulled out some books on Ilidan's history and customs, which he added to my pile. The more I learned, the more overwhelmed I became, and the more respect I felt for Lily, who had studied like this all her life for her role as Talador's next queen. If only I could talk to her now and ask for some guidance.

The library was large and filled to the brim with books of all different types, many more than we had in Talador, and our library wasn't exactly small either. Violet would be delighted to be surrounded by so much knowledge. Someday I'd invite my family to visit me, once relations between our kingdoms had been smoothed out more. Or when Raith finally taught me his damn teleportation spell.

I groaned and rested my head on my arms, which were

folded across a massive tome detailing some wizard war from a thousand years ago. I'd always wanted to learn magic, but never thought it would involve so much reading. I did enjoy reading, but I preferred fiction with romance and adventure, not dry, never-ending historical texts. Perhaps Raith's plan was to drown me in books so he never had to actually teach me magic—or spend time with me at all, for that matter.

Oren eventually saved me by taking me on an afternoon tour of Varlock Castle. In many ways it reminded me of my home with its thick halls, ornate carpets, and high ceilings. But in others it was completely different—the dark stone, the pointed arches, and the large number of torches, candles, and braziers waiting to be lit. It wasn't the foreboding place I'd imagined it to be, though it was still unnervingly empty for a castle.

I did meet most of the staff, who were all polite even if some eyed me with suspicion and others gazed at me with hope. A heavy feeling of responsibility settled over my shoulders, which was entirely new and both unexpected and uncomfortable. These people were under my charge now, relying on me to shape their families' futures. I was never supposed to be a queen, and wasn't at all prepared or qualified for the duty.

We continued the tour and I discovered my absolute favorite part of the castle, the garden outside. Autumn in all its lovely colors had settled over the kingdom already, and the garden was ablaze with red leaves, thick bushes, and hearty flowers. Though Ilidan was a neighbor to Talador, its southern location made it a lot warmer, and I couldn't wait to explore the land. I'd always hated the cold, and delighted in the knowledge that my new home wasn't covered in snow most of the year.

Oren walked beside me down a wide path. "King Raith's great-grandfather built this garden for his wife. Over the years it's changed and grown, with each monarch shaping it to their own tastes."

"It's beautiful," I said. But there was something missing. "I noticed there are no roses in the garden. Wouldn't they grow well in this climate?"

"They would, but King Raith had them all removed after Lady Silena's death three years ago. Roses were her favorite and she often spent many hours tending to them herself." He cleared his throat. "Perhaps you could bring your namesake flowers back to the garden again someday."

I shook my head. "And risk Raith's wrath? I think not."

"His majesty can be...prickly at times, it's true. He's always been a serious sort, and he's gone through a lot these past few years. First the death of his father, followed by the murder of his wife, and then the loss of his mother and his sudden appointment as King. But he has a good heart underneath all those thick layers."

My heart ached for Raith. I couldn't imagine losing everyone I loved in the space of a few years. My sisters were everything to me, and even with this distance between us we would always be close—but Raith was completely alone.

"May I ask what happened to each of them?" I asked.

Oren bowed his head. "Raith's father sacrificed himself at the Battle of Werth to give our soldiers time to escape."

The Battle of Werth was the last major skirmish between our two armies, fought for control of an area on the border between Talador and Ilidan. Both sides took heavy losses and the war became a costly stalemate after that, with neither side gaining much ground in the last six years. It was also the area Raith conceded as part of his negotiations with my father to end the war between the two kingdoms.

"A hero's death," I said, though it saddened me knowing the man had died fighting against my father's army. "And the Queen?"

"She'd been sick for some time, and finally succumbed to her illness two years ago. King Raith was by her side when she passed, at least."

I remembered hearing about that, along with news of the King's coronation. "I'm glad he could be with her at the end."

"Yes, especially since he was still grieving his wife's loss at the time."

I stopped in the middle of the path and turned toward Oren. "How did Raith's wife die? You said she was murdered?"

He hesitated, glancing away. "I should not be the one to tell you this story."

Unease crept over me, but that only made me more determined. "Please, Oren. If I am to be his wife, I must know the truth, and Raith will barely speak to me."

He pressed his lips together, but then nodded. "Lady

Silena was traveling to another part of the kingdom to visit her parents. King Raith—though he was still only a prince then—was supposed to ride with her, but at the last minute he was delayed and told her he would catch up later. Assassins attacked the carriage that night, probably hoping to find him inside, and left her for dead. By the time Raith arrived, it was too late."

"How awful," I said, my chest aching for both Raith and this woman I'd never met. "Do you know who sent the assassins?"

Oren avoided my eyes. "Your father did."

A strangled sound escaped my lips. "My father? How could he have done such a thing?" My hand went to my throat as surprise and horror filled me. "No wonder Raith can barely stand to look at me."

"Raith despises your father, it's true, but he's also blamed himself these past three years for Silena's death. He thinks if he'd been there, he could have saved her."

"Did he love her?" I asked, though I was sure of the answer already.

"Very much."

I nodded, my heart heavy. Marrying for love was almost unheard of for those in a royal family, and he'd been lucky to have had that chance. To then have that love stolen away was the cruelest fate I could have imagined for him. I'd always disliked my father, but now I truly hated him.

Oren bowed his head. "With so much loss in his family, the war with Talador, and...well, other problems...Raith been forced to grow up too fast and his heart has hardened to the world. Everyone here at the castle is hoping you can help him with that."

"Me?" I blinked at Oren. "What am I to do? He will barely even look at me."

"Give him time. He'll come around. He must have chosen you for a reason."

"He didn't choose me. I volunteered."

Oren smiled at me with a twinkle in his eye. "Yes, you did."

He walked down the path with his hands clasped behind his back, while I could only stare after him and ponder his words. Me, help Raith? That seemed unlikely.

I'd always thought the wizard king would be a monster, after all the stories told about him in Talador. After only a day here, I could already tell that wasn't the case, at least not entirely—and I was beginning to wonder if my father was the true monster, after all. Either way, I had a lot to learn about my new husband, even if I would never be able to help him the way Oren wanted.

That night, I donned another gown and made my way to the dining chamber, expecting to see Raith there—but when I entered, I found myself alone except for the servants. I sat at the table and waited for him to arrive, but as my supper was placed in front of me and wine was poured, I knew he wasn't coming.

How was I supposed to help Raith when he wouldn't even face me?

ELEVEN

RAITH

The door to my study banged open and my wife walked into the room, wearing an off-the-shoulder emerald gown while carrying the stack of books I'd given her three days ago. Rose stormed toward me, her amber eyes ablaze, and dropped the books on my desk with a loud *thump*.

"I'm finished," she said.

I arched an eyebrow. "Already?"

She crossed her arms as she stood over me, making my eyes drift to her bare shoulders. "Don't sound so surprised."

I tore my gaze away to glance through the books. "Where's your summary?"

She rolled her eyes. "I'm not doing that. I'll read them, but I'm not writing up a report as if I'm still a child and you're my tutor."

I leaned back in my chair and gave her a level stare. "How am I supposed to know if you actually read them?"

"Perhaps you'd like to quiz me?" She huffed. "I read them. You'll simply have to take my word on it."

I nearly argued the point further, but decided perhaps I had been a tad too harsh in my demands. I slowly rose to my feet and her gaze followed me up as I towered over her. "Fine. No summary. I simply wanted to test your dedication to this endeavor."

Her glare softened and she clasped her hands in front of her. "I'm dedicated, I promise. It's just that I've wanted to learn magic my entire life and I'm ready to get started."

I moved toward another table with a tall stack of books and rested my hand on them. "Then it's time for your next lesson. Now that you understand the history of magic, you must learn the theory. Read these and return once you've finished."

She let out a groan that conjured all sorts of thoughts I shouldn't be having. "More books? Truly, Raith, you must hate me."

Quite the opposite, in fact. If only she knew that at this very moment I was picturing sliding down those off-shoulder sleeves to reveal even more of her skin. With effort, I dragged my eyes away from her tantalizing curves and returned to my desk.

"I have some good news," I said, changing the subject. "Your father has kept his word and has withdrawn his troops from Ilidan's borders. I've ordered our army to retreat as well. The war appears to be well and truly over."

A bright smile lit up her face. "That's wonderful. The people of both kingdoms will be so relieved."

"Indeed. I've already sent out a proclamation announcing the end of the war, along with news of our marriage. Oren has arranged a celebration in the capital later next week, which we must both attend." My mouth twisted. "He's also insisted I host a ball for the nobles later this month."

She nodded. "Both of those are excellent ideas. I'm ready to do whatever is required of me as queen. Is there anything I should do to prepare, or anyone in particular I should know about?"

"Not really. The only nobleman you need to worry about is my cousin, Lord Malren. He's clever, ambitious, narcissistic, and worst of all, next in line for the throne. Watch your back at all times around him, or you might soon find a dagger in it."

"He sounds like a delight. I'll keep an eye out, and on your back as well."

I stiffened at the implication she would look after me. "You need not concern yourself so." I picked up a quill and turned my head to my reports. "I suggest you start reading. Those texts are dense."

She didn't budge. "I will read them on one condition."

"What is it?" I looked up at her again, my eyes narrowing.

"You must join me for supper."

"Tonight?" I usually ate supper in my study, alone. It had been that way ever since Silena was murdered. I couldn't even remember the last time I'd dined in any other part of my castle.

"Tonight, and every night." She raised a hand as I opened my mouth to protest. "I've given up everything from my previous life to become your wife. I've done everything you've wanted of me and will try to be a good queen to your people. I'll read whatever ancient, stuffy books you put in front of me. All I ask is that you share one meal with me a day. That is all."

"Why?" I asked, baffled by her request.

She looked down, and a hint of vulnerability entered her eyes. "I am completely and utterly alone here. I cannot spend my entire life in solitude, and neither can you. If we are to be partners for the rest of our lives, let us at least have supper together every night. Please."

Her plea was too heartfelt for me to ignore and made me realize how unfair I'd been to her all this time. I'd been so focused on how hard this marriage was for me, I didn't realize what toll it was taking on her either. As she'd said, she'd given up everything when she came here, including her entire family and her home. She had to be incredibly lonely here in this dark, foreign castle. I understood loneliness all too well.

"Fine," I said. "I'll see you at supper."

"Thank you." A victorious smile crossed her face as she grasped the books to her ample bosom and left the room in a swish of skirts. My eyes stayed fixed on the doorway long after she'd gone through it, as if hoping she'd return. Sun and Moon, what was I going to do about her?

TWELVE

The castle's staff was even more shocked than I was that Raith had agreed to join me for supper. They flitted about in a frenzy of hushed whispers and clinking silverware as they prepared for his arrival. Oren caught my eye and gave me a knowing smile as he walked by me. I wanted to tell them not to get their hopes up, that it was just supper and nothing more, and Raith might not even arrive after all.

But he did.

At exactly supper time he strode into the private dining chamber, wearing all black as usual. He cut a dashing figure with his tall profile, regal bearing, and the subtle power emanating from him at all times. His commanding presence stole my breath, along with his raven-black hair, storm gray eyes, and the hint of dark stubble across his strong jaw.

For a moment he simply stood in the doorway, taking

me in. I wore the same off-the-shoulder emerald gown from earlier, yet Loura had done my hair in an intricate up-do, topped with a silver and ruby tiara that once belonged to Queen Casnia. A matching necklace adorned my neck and Raith's eyes lingered on it. I hoped he wasn't upset I'd worn his mother's jewels—Oren had brought them to me earlier and suggested I put them on, so I'd thought it was fine. Or was Raith looking at my bare shoulders and the cleavage revealed by the low neckline of my gown? I couldn't tell.

"Rose." He gave me a quick nod as he pulled out my chair for me.

I sank into it with a smile. "Thank you."

He took a seat across from me at the table, which was made of dark wood with intricate designs of swirls and flowers on it. Unlike the grand dining hall, this room was smaller and more intimate, intended for the royal family to share meals together in less formal situations. The servants poured us wine and brought our first course, a soup that smelled of pumpkins and spice, then discreetly disappeared into the adjoining room.

Raith and I began sipping our soup in silence, like two strangers sharing a meal and nothing more. He seemed to have no interest in talking to me, which meant I'd have to be the one to make the effort.

I smiled at him and said, "I truly appreciate this. After spending every meal surrounded by my sisters, I'm not used to eating alone. It's nice to have some company."

"I suppose."

Well, that was enthusiastic. I swirled my spoon through my soup. "Have you no siblings?"

"None. My parents didn't think they could have children for a long time, possibly due to my mother's ongoing health issues. I was an unexpected miracle when she was almost forty years old."

I smiled faintly as I imagined how happy they would have been. "They must have doted on you so much."

"My father taught me magic and my mother taught me to be king." He shrugged. "It was a pleasant childhood overall."

"Did you ever long for siblings?"

"Not particularly, but perhaps you can't miss what you've never had."

"I'm not sure that's true," I said, a lump forming in my throat at the thought of what I'd always missed.

His steely eyes seemed to see right through me. "What did you long for, Rose?"

"My mother. She died giving birth to me. My father remarried many times, but none of his wives lasted long. My sisters and I all learned not to get attached to them. My aunt Dahlia was the closest thing I had to a mother and I love her dearly, but it's not the same."

"I'm guessing your mother was a wizard?"

"She was, and my aunt gave me my mother's spellbook when I came into my magic. I practiced in secret as a way to feel closer to her."

"It's a shame you never had anyone to teach you magic properly."

"But I do now." I raised an eyebrow at him. "Assuming we ever get to actually practice magic, that is."

"Soon, my impatient wife."

His words were almost teasing, but he'd called me his wife, not his apprentice or his queen. I practically glowed from the inside out.

The servants brought out the next course, a chicken dish with an almond sauce, before retreating again. Raith had relaxed significantly, enough to give me the confidence to broach this next topic.

"Oren told me what happened to your late wife," I said.

Raith stiffened, his fingers tightening around his knife. "Did he now?"

"I know this is a difficult subject, but I felt I had a right to know, so please don't be upset with him. I won't pry into your past any further." I smoothed my hands on my napkin. "All I wish to say is that I am truly sorry for what my father did. I also want you to know that he never told any of us about what he'd done. If I'd known he could do such despicable things..." I shook my head as emotion gripped my throat. "It is inexcusable and I'm so sorry for your loss."

Raith set down his knife, and when he met my eyes, he didn't look angry. "You do not need to apologize. I don't blame you or your sisters for what your father has done. If anything, I pity that you had to live under his thumb for so long."

"It wasn't so bad. He was distant and sometimes cold, but never hurt us in any way. He was harder on me than the others, but I could take it. However, I'm beginning to realize how sheltered I was while in his castle. I can only wonder what else he hid from us about the war's atrocities, or what other false tales he allowed to spread. You should hear what they say about you in Talador."

"Oh, I'm well aware." Raith's long fingers traced the edge of his wine glass. "I don't hold it against you. We both inherited this war from our parents. Neither one of us wanted it, and now we're stuck with the consequences."

"But we ended the war too." I reached across and rested my hand on his, touching him for the first time since our wedding. His eyes widened slightly, but he didn't pull away.

"Yes, we did. I am grateful to you for that."

"You're the one who came to my father, despite what he did. It must have been difficult for you to face him, knowing he was responsible for your wife's death. I'm in awe of your bravery and dedication to your people."

"More like desperation," Raith said. "We could not have survived another winter at war with Talador."

"Nor could we." I squeezed his hand slightly. "Our kingdoms have hated each other for a long time and many terrible things were done these last few years. There is nothing we can do about that now, but perhaps our legacy will be one of peace and not war. Perhaps the next generation will grow up with our two kingdoms as allies and not enemies."

"Perhaps," he said, but he didn't sound optimistic. As he slid his hand away from mine, his face darkened.

"What is it, Raith?" For once it had seemed like we were connecting, but now he had withdrawn again.

He ran a weary hand over his face. "My apologies. I'm simply tired. The last few days have been especially busy."

"Is there anything I can do to help? Perhaps I can ease your burden in some way, or…"

He rose to his feet, leaving the rest of his food untouched. "There is nothing you can do. Now if you'll excuse me, I have some business to attend to tonight."

"Tonight?" I blinked at him. "But it's already dark."

"Indeed, it is." He gave me a quick nod, then turned to leave. "Good night, Rose."

I stared at my food for another few minutes after he was gone, but my appetite had vanished. Yes, he'd joined me for supper, but I'd expected him to stay for the entire meal, at least. What could he possibly have to do now that was so important? Curiosity and annoyance spurred me to my feet, and I followed in the direction he'd gone, likely back to his study. I heard movement coming from the room and quickened my steps. Yet when I entered, he was already gone, teleporting somewhere else with only a thought.

But where?

THIRTEEN

RAITH

I teleported into the center of Haversham and gazed at the stone buildings in dismay as thick darkness crept over them. I'd received a report this morning that the small town was being attacked by shadows again, but it was much worse than I'd expected—or perhaps it had escalated faster than usual this time.

Thick, inky darkness swallowed one side of the town completely with long shadowy tendrils stretching out from it, roping around columns, climbing up walls, and creeping into windows. Within hours the entire town would be lost unless I did something to stop it. Unless I fought it back, as I'd done every night in various parts of my kingdom for the last two years.

I called forth runes to summon lightning and struck at the black, oozing darkness covering the buildings. The shadows shuddered and made a sound like a whine, but a few of the tendrils burned up and turned to smoke. Others retreated, reluctantly drawing back to the main body of darkness, which they were absorbed into. I struck again and again, lighting up the night until it was as bright as day. Only then did the heavy shadows begin to burn away.

And then the nightmare beasts came.

Inky black monsters from the Shadow Lands slithered, flew, crawled, and galloped through the cobblestone streets, taking on all different forms. I cast my own runes of darkness and took hold of the beasts, sending them back to their world. I called forth fire and burned them to ashes. I threw lightning until they dissolved into smoke. But they kept coming, filling the night with piercing howls as shadows curled away from their bodies, leaving a trail of darkness in their wake. One scratched ice-cold fangs against my arm while another tore at my cloak with claws coated in black tar. Each time I sent one back to the abyss, another one took its place, over and over. Until finally none stood before me.

When the town was silent and empty again, I reached out to the darkness covering the buildings, bending it to my will, forcing it to retreat. Sweat dripped down my forehead, my stomach ached with hunger, and exhaustion made my limbs weary, but I couldn't leave until this town was safe, even if the darkness would likely return in a few days. No matter how much I fought it, or how hard I pushed it back, it always returned—and even stronger than before.

With a shudder, the darkness finally relented and sank in on itself, until it was simply gone. When the town was only as dark as night, I leaned against the nearest stone wall and tried to catch my breath and steady my shaking hands. Weariness crept over me, along with a sense of hopelessness and the burden of failure, despite my small victory tonight. The town had already been evacuated, likely abandoned forever, and I couldn't blame them. So many of my people had lost their homes and even their lives to the Shadow Lord's assault. Villages were vanishing every day and there was little I could do to stop it.

Rose might be able to assist me with her own magic once she was trained, but my heart clenched at the very thought. Even the notion of putting her in danger was intolerable. No, I had to keep her as far away from this threat as possible. The less she knew about it, the better.

"Come out and face me," I growled to the Shadow Lord, though I knew he wouldn't listen. He must have some qualm with me to attack my kingdom over the last few years, not just with his beasts and his darkness, but in person. I wasn't sure why he stalked my lands, and I'd never seen him myself, but reports all described him the same: a massive, shadowy figure with pointed wings who cast black ink from his claws that quickly crept over everything in its path. He was responsible for this plague of darkness, but I didn't know why he'd targeted us. Or how to stop him.

Once I regained a touch of my strength I walked through the town, searching for any clues as to why it had been attacked or how to stop the Shadow Lord and his minions. As usual, I found nothing. My kingdom was running out of time, and I was no closer to discovering a solution than I'd been two years ago.

Bitter frustration tore through me as I teleported back to my study with my last ounce of strength. I stumbled toward my chaise lounge, but paused when I saw Rose sleeping upon it, still in her far-too-alluring gown and wearing my mother's jewels. Temptation urged me to run a finger along her bare shoulder, to wake her up with a soft kiss on the graceful slope of her neck, but of course I resisted.

What was she doing in my study? Was she waiting for my return? Perhaps she'd been upset at my sudden departure during supper. I'd shared a meal with her for as long as I could, despite her probing questions about my past, but when true night fell, I had work to do and couldn't delay any longer. Work she could never know about.

I ran a ragged hand through my hair as I gazed at her. I usually passed out as soon as I returned from my nightly battles, but tonight she was in the way. An image crossed my mind of me curling up beside her, wrapping my arms around her, and pulling her body against mine, but I banished it immediately. Instead I gathered her up in my arms and lifted her carefully, my willpower momentarily overcoming my exhaustion.

She stirred slightly as she melted against me, turning into my embrace as if she belonged there, and rested her fingers on my chest. I inhaled sharply when she nuzzled her face into my neck, and I breathed in her sweet scent. Her beautiful, trusting face tilted up at me, her eyes still heavy with sleep, and a large, gaping hole opened in my chest. She made me feel all sorts of complicated, horrible things I usually kept locked deep inside. Loneliness. Longing.

Desire. And something else, something I refused to even name. Something I could never feel again.

With a grunt, I tightened my grip on her soft curves and carried her out of the study through the brightly-lit halls, past the few guards who stood watch. So far, the castle had been spared most of the Shadow Lord's wrath, though he had been spotted nearby a few times. I suspected he was waiting until I'd truly hit the end of my limits protecting my kingdom, and then he would swoop in and destroy me completely, taking everything I still held dear. Including Rose.

I wouldn't let that happen.

With a reserve of strength I didn't even know I had, I managed to carry my wife up the stairs and kicked open the door to her rooms. I hadn't been in the royal consort's chambers in years and was surprised to find they hadn't changed much, though Rose had put her a few of her things about the room. Her mother's old spellbook. A few trinkets she'd brought from home. A brush and a bottle of perfume. Nothing that marked this as her permanent home, not yet. As if she were still a guest here and not the lady of this castle. Not that I blamed her. It had only been a few days, after all. But I found myself hoping she would settle in and come to accept this as her new home soon.

I set her down gently on the large bed, but her fingers tightened on my shirt as if she was unwilling to let me go or wanted to pull me into bed with her. All those thoughts I'd tried to banish earlier came rushing back as I imagined how easy it would be to give in to her.

"Raith," she said, her eyes fluttering open. The sound of my name on her lips did terrible things to me. Terrible, wonderful things.

"Shh." I pushed a piece of silky hair back from her face before I realized what I was doing. I quickly yanked my hand away. "Go back to sleep."

Her hands released my shirt, but then went to her neck, where my mother's jewels were still draped across her collar. "Help me take these off."

I removed her tiara first, before lifting her up just enough so I could unclasp the necklace. My hands brushed against her soft skin, and she let out a light sigh at my touch.

"I won't wear them again," she said as she climbed under the blankets, even though she was still fully dressed. Her eyes were hooded, her words heavy with sleep, which threatened to quickly claim her again.

"Why wouldn't you?" I reached under the blankets to grab hold of her slippers and remove them. I tried to make the gesture as innocent as possible, but still felt a rush of heat as I touched her bare ankles. It had been way too long since I'd been with a woman if even her ankles, of all things, turned me on.

"The way you looked at me earlier..." She turned her head away with a sigh. "I'm sorry. I shouldn't have worn your mother's jewels."

My back stiffened. "Don't be. They're yours now. I wasn't upset. If anything, I was taken back by how beautiful you looked wearing them."

"Truly?" The sleepy smile that slid across her lips made

my trousers even more uncomfortable. "Then why did you leave?"

"I had business to attend to in another town. You shouldn't have waited up for me." I tucked the blankets around her. "Go to sleep, Rose."

Her eyes were already closed, and I wondered if she had fallen asleep already. Before I could stop myself, I bent down and pressed a soft kiss to the top of her head. I straightened up quickly, wondering what on earth had gotten into me. With any luck, she wouldn't remember I had done something so foolish tomorrow.

I quickly made my escape, using the adjoining door to stumble into my bedroom as the exhaustion caught up to me. I hadn't slept in my own bed in days, perhaps weeks, but I had no other choice tonight. I collapsed onto it still in my clothes, and was instantly sucked into dark, dreamless sleep.

FOURTEEN

ROSE

My next few days were spent with my nose in the books Raith had given me or being fitted by a seamstress and her team in beautiful, elaborate gowns for my upcoming debut as Ilidan's queen. The only time I saw Raith was at supper, which he always attended for a short while before abruptly making an excuse and dashing from the room. Every night he teleported somewhere, doing something he refused to speak about, and my mind ran wild, conjuring up different scenarios to explain his late-night escapades. I imagined him sneaking into an illicit gambling hall, or meeting with a group of assassins to plot and scheme, or, worst of all, climbing into the bed of his mistress. A lump formed in my throat at that last thought.

But then I remembered the way he'd carried me up the stairs the other night and tucked me into bed. His touch had been so tender, and even in my half-asleep state his low voice had seemed to wrap around me like a warm blanket. Sometimes I fancied he might have said I was beautiful and then kissed my forehead, but I quickly dismissed that as wishful thinking and nothing more.

Raith had been distant ever since that night and especially quiet at supper, no matter how much I tried to initiate conversation. To break the tense silence, I told him about each of my sisters, about Dahlia's secret room in the castle, about the striped cat I had growing up named Whiskers, and a dozen other things about myself that he probably had little interest in. And every time he left me alone halfway through our meal I wondered, why did I even bother?

Once I finally finished Raith's latest pile of books, I searched him out and found him in his study. The door was slightly ajar and I paused before entering, letting my eyes linger on his profile. He stood over a large tome, his head bent in concentration, a strand of black hair falling over his brow. I'd caught him in a rare, unguarded moment, and my heart ached at the sight. I found myself holding my breath, hoping to delay him noticing me so I could drink in the sight of him a little while longer. It was such an unexpected pleasure to be able to stare at him as long as I liked without his disapproving gray eyes piercing right through me. Instead I could simply let my gaze rest on his sharp jaw, which was dusted with a light coat of stubble that crept down his neck and into the high collar of his black cloak. I imagined trailing my fingers down it and wondered what it would feel like against my skin. Or my tongue...

Raith's head jerked toward me, his eyes narrowing. "Yes?"

And just like that, the moment was ruined.

I straightened up, hoping he couldn't tell what I'd been thinking about from my flushed cheeks or slightly parted lips, then crossed the room to his desk. I set down the stack of books I'd completely forgotten I was holding while I'd been gaping at him. "I'm finished with your latest round of busywork. Do you have another stack of books ready for me?"

"Perhaps." One of his perfect, dark eyebrows lifted up. "What was your analysis of what you read?"

"Beyond the fact that each one was a total bore..." I tilted my head as I considered. "Some wizards theorize that magic was given to us by the Sun and Moon to protect and guide the people, while others claim it was meant for us to rule with. But from what I read, the Six Kingdoms have been at war as far back as history has been recorded, and in many cases magic only made things worse, not better. Magic is not a gift, but a responsibility."

He leaned against his desk, crossing his arms as he appraised me. "A sound analysis. As you said, magic is not to be used lightly, and those who have it can shape the world, but perhaps they shouldn't. We must always be careful how we use our magic, especially since we are already in a position of power and privilege. Do you see now why I wanted you to understand that?"

"You don't want me to be reckless or overconfident. Or

to think that using magic can solve every problem. Or to become a tyrant intent on conquering other kingdoms like my father."

"Indeed." His intelligent gray eyes stared at me so long I thought he must be reading my thoughts or peering deep into my soul. "Perhaps you're ready for the next lesson."

He straightened up and walked out of the room without another word. I grabbed my skirts and followed him like a puppy tailing its master and hoping for a treat. He'd likely hand me another massive pile of thick, dusty history books, but maybe I could convince him to show me a new rune also. Just one, at least. I would take anything at this point.

He strode into his magical workshop and I hurried a little faster. The door slammed shut behind us, making me jump, and then we were surrounded by all of his books, flasks, and other artifacts. Every time I entered this room, I sensed all the things I didn't know yet, the runes I could learn, and the vast potential I wanted nothing more than to unlock.

He moved to one side of the room and scanned the bookshelf with the skull on it, while I practically quivered with anticipation. When he grabbed a thick book, my heart sank a little, even though it was what I'd been expecting. But instead of handing it to me, he opened it on the table in the center and flipped to a page about halfway through.

"There," he said, pointing to something on the page. "This is the spell you cast the first time we met."

I moved up behind him to peer down at the book. The

pages were old and filled with runes, the intricate designs done in black ink with a heavy hand. Excitement rose up within me. This book was even bigger than my mother's spellbook and must hold so many runes I didn't know yet. "Yes, that's the one."

"Cast it again now."

I drew in a surprised breath and took a few steps back, before raising my hand to trace the shape of the rune. Silvery light followed my fingers as the power grew within me and the ice shard formed in the air.

"No, no, no," Raith said, holding up a hand to stop me.

My fingers froze and the half-finished shard vanished, disintegrating into nothing. "What's wrong?"

"Everything." He pinched the bridge of his nose. "First of all, your execution is incorrect. Study the rune again and make sure to get it right next time. And second, you're trying to form the rune with your hand, instead of with your mind."

My brow furrowed. "I don't see how there is a difference."

"Of course you don't." He huffed. "Watch me."

He slowly and very deliberately cast the same rune I'd been practicing, except the silvery light was stronger, emanating with his intense, controlled power. Sun and Moon, his magic was strong. I'd once heard his only equal was the Archwizard herself, and now I truly believed it.

At the end of his rune he added a small circle, and the magic flashed bright before shifting into a perfect, ornate snowflake hovering between us. The icicles were so delicate, the design so elaborate, I couldn't imagine how he had created something so beautiful out of nothing but his own magic and willpower.

"Each rune is simply a base spell," he said, as he drew more runes, creating different snowflakes in the air, each one unique. He moved gracefully, almost as if he were a painter and the world his canvas, and soon the room glittered with frost and ice. "Once you understand the various complexities of the symbols involved, you can change them to suit your will. Add a flourish here, subtract a line there, and so forth. But the runes are not what really matters—it's all about intent. The runes are simply a way for you to channel your magic into something more specific and precise."

I reached out to touch the nearest snowflake, enchanted by its beauty, but it crumbled away when my fingers brushed against it. I'd studied magic for years on my own, but had never been able to make anything like that before. My runes were crude compared to what Raith could do.

Humbled, I bowed my head. "What must I do?"

He ran a hand along his stubbled jaw as he considered me, then grabbed something off the table. A long strip of black cloth.

"I'm going to put this over your eyes," he said, as he stepped toward me.

My heart jumped into my throat, but I nodded. He moved behind me, brushing my hair out of the way, and I shivered slightly at his light touch. As he wrapped the silky black cloth around my head and plunged me into darkness, I remembered tales I'd heard of men and women doing this sort of thing in more...intimate ways. Heat rushed between my legs as he tied the knot behind my head, while I imagined what he might do to me next. How his hands might travel down my body...

"Now," he said, his voice right at my ear. "Cast the rune."

I quickly banished those sensual thoughts from my mind. All Raith wanted was a student, nothing more. I couldn't let myself forget that, because when I did it only hurt more once I was reminded of the truth.

I willed my hand to be steady as I began to trace the rune from memory. I tried to put as much power and grace into it as Raith had done, but doubt and uncertainty crept in and I knew my sad attempt at a snowflake looked nothing as fine as his. When my arm dropped, I didn't even need to take off the blindfold to know I'd failed.

"This isn't working," I said.

"Have some patience. That's half your problem."

Now he sounded like Lily. I was about to bite out a reply, when his cool fingers wrapped around my wrist, making me jump. He moved behind me, his hard chest pressed against my back, as he raised my arm up.

"We'll do it together." His hand slid over mine, guiding my index finger. My heart pounded so loud I was sure he could hear it, and all I could think about was how close he was to me. How he was touching me with a firm, yet gentle grip. How he smelled like sparks and shadows. Surely it would be impossible for me to cast anything like this, especially as all the torrid thoughts returned in full force. I wanted nothing more than to learn back into his chest and nuzzle against him, they way I'd done when he'd carried me to bed the other night.

But as we began tracing the rune, my lack of vision helped me focus my mind until there was nothing but me and him and the magic. It surged between us, swelling and growing eagerly like a bonfire jumping to life, filling me with power. I gasped as the spell flowed out of us together, forming a silver rune so bright it shone through the blindfold. When he released my wrist, I tugged the cloth down to see a snowflake hovering before us that was larger and even more beautiful and complex than any of the ones he'd done.

"Nice work." His breath tickled my neck. "Your magic is stronger than I expected."

Was it? His praise glowed within me like an ember on a cold day. I turned my head toward him, my lips dangerously close to his mouth. "Thank you."

He lingered there for a breath, his eyes searching mine, the moment thick with anticipation. But then he quickly stepped back, and the connection between us was immediately severed. "Don't thank me yet. You still have a long way to go."

"I'm willing to do whatever it takes."

He waved his hand dismissively. "Then do it again."

I cast the frost rune a dozen more times, but it was never the same as when we'd performed the spell together. Conjuring magic together had been intoxicating. Was that what it felt like every time Raith used his magic? I couldn't imagine having all that raw power inside me trying to get out, and admired his control. Or was the magic stronger because we'd been doing it together?

When Raith was satisfied with my progress, he closed the large book with a snap, sending a cloud of dust into the air. "Take this book and practice the runes in the first chapter every single day. Do it in a secluded area of the garden where you can't hurt anyone with your floundering."

My eyebrows darted up. "Does that mean I'm allowed to leave the castle alone now? Has the threat passed?"

"During the day, yes. But don't leave the castle grounds."

"I understand," I said solemnly, though inside I was jumping up and down like a child about to get cake. "And after I finish the first chapter?"

"When I decide you're ready, we'll start on the second one."

I nodded and took the book, excited to pore through it and begin my true magical studies. As I held it against my chest like the precious gift it was, I couldn't help but smile as I walked to the door. There was a lot of work ahead of me, but I looked forward to it. Not only because I was finally fulfilling my dream of following in my mother's footsteps and becoming a wizard, but because magic was one of the few things Raith and I had in common. The one thing binding us together other than our unfortunate circumstances and the sins of our forefathers. If that was all I would ever get from Raith, I would savor each moment of it.

At the door I turned back to him. "Is it always like that when you use your magic?" I asked, before I could change my mind. "Or was it...different with the two of us?"

He stared at me so long I worried he might not answer, before he finally said, "No, it's not always like that."

FIFTEEN

Oren lunged toward me with his blade and I parried the blow, spinning away from him. My arm ached and my shoulders were stiff; I'd gone too long between practices and was paying for it. The sound of clashing swords filled the air as we sparred on the trodden grass on the edge of the garden, our battle hidden by a tall, thick hedge.

With a quick move, Oren disarmed me and flashed me a triumphant smile. I sighed as I stepped back and rolled my shoulders while sweat dripped down my forehead. Oren's lined face was flushed as he grabbed a flask and chugged some water. It was an unusually hot day for this time of year, and we were both wilting a little because of it.

"Can't you magic away this weather?" Oren asked, as he closed the flask.

I yanked my black shirt off and used it to wipe my face, before tossing it aside. "And defy the Sun god? I think not."

He snorted. "The gods gave you magic for a reason. Surely you can use it to spare an old man a heat stroke."

I picked my sword up off the ground. "Not a chance. I might actually defeat you if that happens."

He got into his fighting stance, his body still agile despite his age. "Unlikely. Not if you keep neglecting to practice."

I gripped my sword tighter. "I've been a little busy."

"Indeed," he said, his voice heavy with disapproval. For what now, I wondered? I was sure he had a long list of areas where I was falling short.

"Is everything ready for the celebration tomorrow?" I asked, as our swords met again.

"Of course." He sniffed, as if he was offended I was even asking.

"And the ball?"

"Everything is in order." He paused, his mouth curling in distaste. "Your cousin has accepted the invitation."

"A pity, but not a surprise. He'll want to see if my new wife is a threat to him."

He dodged my next blow easily. "And is she?"

"Most definitely."

We finished that round with another point going to Oren, to no one's surprise. He'd taught me everything I knew about using a sword from the time I was a child. I preferred to use magic, but it was prudent to have many ways to defend yourself and those one was responsible for. Not that it had helped me protect Silena, but that only spurred me to practice harder.

As I wiped sweat off my brow, I caught sight of Rose

standing to the side, staring at me as if she'd never seen me before. Staring at my bare chest, to be precise. Her cheeks were flushed, though I had a feeling that wasn't from the heat, and a rush of lust rolled through me at the way her thin gown hugged her hips and her ample breasts. Our gazes locked and heat passed between us, and I became aware of how much I wanted her, and how I could tell she wanted me too.

"What are you doing here?" I asked, my voice rough.

The heat in her eyes flared into annoyance. "Finding a secluded place to cast spells in the garden, as you told me to do. I heard some noises here and thought to investigate. The better question is, what are you doing?" Her eyes dropped to my chest again, like she couldn't help herself, and I got a tiny glimpse of her tongue as it ran across her lower lips.

"Practicing, obviously," I said, trying not to let show what the sight of her pink tongue did to me. Needless to say, my trousers were a lot tighter than they'd been a minute ago.

She crossed her arms. "It looked like Oren was practicing, and you were getting smacked on your rear."

My eyes narrowed. "And it looked like you were staring at my chest instead of doing magic."

Her arms dropped. "I most definitely was not! I was simply blinded by your pale skin and had to stop to shade my eyes from it."

"More like you were wondering what else I could do with a sword." I slid my blade into my sheath slowly and deliberately, while her eyes widened.

Oren cleared his throat. "My queen, was there something you needed? I think we're about finished here."

"No, I'm quite all right. You can carry on playing with your big sticks." She cast me one last look that was something between amused and irritated, before taking her skirts in hand and continuing on her stroll. The path twisted around a hedge, and within seconds she'd vanished from sight. I found myself wishing she'd return, while also feeling relieved she was gone.

I let out a long breath and wiped my forehead again, feeling ten times hotter than when I'd been sparring. Rose had the ability to make my blood boil like no one else could. And not just with anger either.

"It seems the two of you are getting along then," Oren said, with a knowing smile. "Ah, I remember when my wife would look at me like that. Sun and Moon, I miss her."

I grabbed my shirt off the grass. "I don't know what you're talking about."

"Don't play the fool with me." He rested a hand on my shoulder. "Most men in your position would consider themselves lucky. Is it truly so terrible to desire your wife?"

My back stiffened. "It is when you're still mourning your former wife."

A look of pity crossed his lined face. "Oh, Raith. Silena would want you to be happy. It's time for you to move on."

"I don't see you moving on and finding another wife."

"I'm a crusty old man with a son your age. You're a king in the prime of his life."

I shook my head. "Now is not a good time for romance. Maybe someday...but only once things are safer in Ilidan."

Oren pursed his lips, but then nodded. "How is the magical training coming along?"

"She's more powerful than I expected, but rash and inexperienced. She has no patience and wants to skip ahead to the most powerful runes without learning the basics first."

"And she's as stubborn as you are," he pointed out.

"Well, yes."

Oren chuckled. "I remember a young lad who would follow his father everywhere and beg him to teach him some new runes. He certainly wasn't patient either."

I cast a spell to refill both of our flasks with more water. "I was a child. She is not."

"Perhaps you should remember that as well. You can't teach her the way your father taught you."

I gave him a stern look. "I think I know the best way to train her in the magical arts."

He shrugged. "If she's as strong as you say, it would be in our best interests to train her quickly. We could use her in the fight against the Shadow Lord."

"No." The word came out more vehemently than I'd intended. "I will not risk her life. Not now. Not ever."

A smug expression crossed Oren's face. "Ah, so you do care about her."

I paused as conflicting emotions stirred inside me. Obviously, I cared about her. I would not train her in magic otherwise. But things with Rose were...complicated. "She is my wife," I simply said.

While Oren returned to the castle, I found Rose in another part of the garden, her face twisted in concentration as she traced a rune to conjure fire. Her power flared, sparking bright as flames burst to life from a cluster of twigs. I nearly conjured more water in case I needed to douse the flames, but she managed to keep them under control. Barely.

"You seem to have an affinity for fire," I said.

She quickly turned toward me, startled. "Do you think so?"

I nodded as I moved toward her. "No wonder you had such trouble with frost."

She let out a surprised laugh as she pushed back her long, dark hair. "One would think frost was in my blood and not fire, after growing up in the frozen north."

"Rose, no one would ever mistake you for anything but fiery."

A small smile touched her lips, before she wiped at her brow. "Perhaps, although in that case I should be able to handle this weather better. It rarely gets this warm in Talador, especially in the fall. I'm not used to it at all."

"Make sure you drink plenty of water and you'll be fine." I gestured toward the space where she'd been practicing. "Show me what you've been doing."

With a wry smile she turned and began casting her runes, her movements quicker and more confident than they'd been before, which in turn made her spells more powerful. In the three days since we'd cast snowflakes in my workshop, she must have worked hard at this. She was a much stronger wizard than I'd imagined, and as I watched her bend and twist the flames to her will, something like pride filled my chest.

"Yes, definitely a fire affinity," I said, with a quick nod.

"What is your affinity?" she asked, as she took a break to drink some water.

Sweat gleamed on her chest above her low neckline in a most distracting way. I forced myself not to stare, even if the sight of her full breasts rising and falling with each breath was hard not to admire. "I have two. Lightning and shadow."

"Two?" Her eyebrows darted up. "I didn't realize that was possible."

"It's rare. I've only heard of a few others with two affinities."

"Including the Archwizard?"

"Indeed. Her affinities are wind and stone. A powerful combination."

"It must be wonderful to have two," she said, as she easily conjured a ball of fire and made it jump from one hand to the other.

"It is, but with more power comes a heavier burden." If not for my affinities, the Shadow Lord might not have targeted my kingdom at all. I'd gladly give them up to protect my people, without question.

"Oh Raith, always so solemn." She lightly brushed her fingers against my jaw, igniting a flame inside me. "At least admit you enjoy the power a little."

I nearly leaned into her touch, so desperate for more of it after being starved of any intimate contact for years. Instead, I summoned my willpower and stepped back. "Magic is a responsibility, not something to be enjoyed. Continue practicing. We have the royal procession tomorrow, but the next morning I want to see what you've learned."

She gave me an overly dramatic curtsey, giving me another glimpse of her ample cleavage. "Yes, master," she said, her voice dripping with sarcasm. "Is there anything else you require?"

"No. That will be all."

I turned to leave, but spotted a bead of sweat dripping down her neck, and cast a quick spell. Clouds gathered in the sky above us, blocking out the sun and instantly cooling the air by a few degrees. If she was going to practice fire, at least she wouldn't overheat or become dehydrated at the same time.

Dammit, maybe I cared about her a little too much.

SIXTEEN

ROSE

I adjusted the heavy crown on my head, which kept slipping to the side, while the open carriage rumbled through the cobblestone streets. My gown was even heavier than the crown, with a tight bodice that flared into many layers of skirts the color of red wine, adorned with black embroidered roses with vines and tiny thorns. I loved how it combined the style that was popular in Ilidan at the moment with a touch of me as well. For the first time, I truly felt like a queen.

As for Raith, he looked stunning in black and white beside me, his head held high. His crown was a larger version of mine: shining silver with large red rubies. Every inch of him radiated power, confidence, and elegance. It was hard to take my eyes off him, and I only hoped I looked half as regal as he did.

I managed to tear my eyes from Raith as the procession

moved forward. The crowd surged on either side of the road, and I gazed across more faces than I had ever seen in one place before. It seemed the entire population of Archdale, the capital of Ilidan, had turned out for the royal celebration today.

"What do you think of the city?" Raith asked.

"It's lovely." And it was. Even with the crowd flooding the streets, I could tell the city was clean and well-maintained, despite being one of the oldest ones in Ilidan. It was obviously prosperous as well, likely bolstered by the trade brought in from the river, which wound its way throughout the capital like a snake.

I studied the stone buildings around us, each one with a torch or brazier in front of it waiting to be lit after the sun went down. Trees covered in red and brown leaves lined the streets, with silver garland strung between them in honor of the celebration today. The cheering crowd threw red rose petals and star-shaped confetti at us, and I waved and smiled, while Raith sat stoically beside me. This was my first visit to Archdale, and while I would have preferred doing it with a lot less fanfare, I wanted to soak in as much of it as I could.

The procession stretched both ahead of our carriage and behind us, down the twisting roads of the city. Dozens of dancers, musicians, and other entertainers celebrated the end of the war and the announcement of our marriage with song and flashes of bright color. Guards were stationed everywhere, moving along with the carriage on foot and on horseback, but Raith didn't seem overly concerned. I supposed when you were a powerful wizard king you had little to fear.

"Your people seem to love you." I nodded toward the banners proclaiming *Long live King Raith!* Others praised the Sun and Moon, and even more celebrated the end of the war. I even spotted one or two that welcomed me to Ilidan.

He shrugged. "Perhaps."

"They do. You'd never see this kind of celebration in Talador for our king. The people feel he's abandoned them. But you ended a war. You're a hero."

"I've simply tried to do my best for my kingdom," Raith said. "I'm sure there are many areas in which I've failed miserably. Or other problems I can't seem to solve."

"Raith, you've done a wonderful job, especially considering how young you were when you became king, and all the other things you've had to deal with." I lightly touched his arm. "I'm proud to be your wife and queen."

He cocked his head. "Truly?"

I smiled at him. "Truly."

He gazed at me in a way that made the rest of the world fade away. I couldn't hear the crowd or see the banners, the only thing that existed was the way his gray eyes captured mine. Something passed between us, an understanding laced with temptation and heat, but then we turned a corner and the carriage jolted, and the moment was lost.

The crowd on this street wasn't throwing confetti. There were no bright banners or loud cheers. The mood had suddenly gone from celebratory to hostile as we rolled down the street. Men and women in the front line of the crowd shook their heads, crossed their arms, or glared at us. No, at *me*.

"Go back to the frozen lands!" one man yelled, and a moment later something sharp hit my arm, making me yelp. A rock.

Raith's eyes darkened, storm clouds gathered, and thunder rumbled in the sky. Lightning crackled in his palms and a few people gasped. He glared out at the crowd with cold fury, as if searching for the one who'd struck me. I'd never seen that look on his face before, but I wasn't afraid. If anything, I was surprised—and a little thrilled—he'd be so protective of me.

"It's all right." I rested a hand on his knee. "We knew some people wouldn't be happy about our marriage. Not when our kingdoms have been at war for so long."

His eyes narrowed. "You're their queen. They should respect you."

"Maybe they will someday. I haven't done anything to earn that respect yet."

"We ended the war with our marriage. Is that not enough?" He scowled, but the sparks in his hands vanished. "I suppose you're right. Our kingdoms have been enemies for decades. Many people lost loved ones to the war. It will take time to heal those old wounds."

"Exactly. This is only the first step." I slid my fingers into his, which still tingled with power. "Showing the people that we're one united front will prove this alliance is real and that things will change for our people."

"You are very wise, my queen." He raised my hand and

pressed a kiss to my knuckles, sending a slight shiver up my spine. A few people in the crowd cheered at the sight. I knew he'd done it just for them, but it still made me want more.

I flashed him a bright smile and then turned it onto the crowd as we continued down the winding streets toward our destination, the Sun and Moon Temple on the western side of Archdale. The buildings grew older as we approached, and I caught sight of something painted on the side of them. Warnings drawn with bold, dark strokes that proclaimed: *Beware the night, stay in the light.*

"What is that about?" I asked, gesturing toward the wall.

Raith's face turned hard at the sight. "Nothing you need to concern yourself with."

I tugged my hand away from him. "Don't tell me that. I want to concern myself with it." We passed another warning: *Fear the darkness, Sun and Moon protect us.* "What are these people afraid of? Does it have something to do with how bright the castle is kept at night? And why I'm not allowed to step outside after sundown?"

Raith's eyebrows pinched together. "We'll discuss it later, Rose. Now is not the time."

I was ready to demand he tell me everything immediately, but we were nearly to the temple now. This discussion would have to wait, even though I was impatient to get the truth. I was on the brink of discovering the answer to questions I'd had the entire time I'd lived in Ilidan, and I wouldn't let Raith keep secrets from me any longer.

The long procession finally culminated at the temple,

BEAUTY IN DARKNESS   113

which consisted of an area open to the sky with tall pillars and arches. Behind this courtyard stood a large building made of the same glittering black stone as Varlock Castle, with gold and silver carvings of the Celestials all over it.

When our carriage stopped, Raith stepped down and offered me his hand to help me out, which was no easy feat in this voluminous gown. The crowd cheered as we walked up the steps to the temple hand in hand, although one man spat at my feet, barely missing my slipper. Guards held him back while Raith's fingers clenched tight around mine, but I kept my head up and continued walking. Despite my brave face and my words to Raith earlier, it still stung knowing some people didn't like me or approve of me as his wife. It was to be expected, of course, but it was still hard to be the object of such animosity—and a reminder that we had a lot to do before our two kingdoms could truly be at peace.

At the top of the steps, the elderly female priest gave us both a warm smile, her eyes twinkling. The sun had nearly set and was casting us in the deep purple hues of twilight. All major ceremonies were performed at dawn or dusk, the holiest times of day when the Celestials were a little closer to each other. The only more auspicious times were eclipses, which were sacred holidays in all the Six Kingdoms.

The priest performed a long blessing on both of us, her voice carrying out across the crowd as night fell and the Sun passed control to the Moon. When it was finished, she nodded to both of us and stepped back with a low bow.

Raith caught my eye and gave my hand a squeeze, before turning to the crowd gathered upon the steps and through the street. Hundreds of people stared up at us, some with hatred, some with fear, and some with awe or relief. *My* people now, I realized with a lump in my throat.

Raith raised his hand and cast a spell that amplified his voice so it spread throughout the city. "My good citizens of Ilidan, it is my greatest pleasure to announce that the long war between our kingdom and Talador is over. King Balsam has removed his troops from our borders, and I have called back our army as well. After decades at war, our kingdoms are finally at peace."

The audience burst into cheers and applause, drowning out anything he might have said next. He paused as he waited for the response to die down, then turned toward me and took my hand again.

"I have this woman to thank for our newfound peace," he said. "Princess Rose of Talador volunteered to marry me to end the war started by our forefathers and to unite our kingdoms despite our differences. Both of us are committed to making this alliance work, and though we'll never be able to make up for what was lost during the many years at war, we hope we can bring forth a new era of prosperity and stability to Ilidan. I'm proud to present her to you as your new queen." He raised our hands above our heads. "Together, the two of us shall fight back the darkness covering our land!"

Although my smile was genuine as we faced the crowd, I couldn't help but wonder about his last sentence and what he meant by it. The crowd roared even louder, clapping and stomping their boots, and I didn't hear any booing this time. Perhaps his speech had won a few of the doubters over.

Raith raised his other hand and magic danced across the sky, with pinpricks of bright light bursting into vibrant colors that formed different designs, including a rose, a bolt of lightning, and the symbols of the Celestials. An awed hush fell over the crowd as he worked, and with his other hand still entwined with mine, I felt the power thrumming through him. I sensed when he cast each rune and saw the symbol in my mind as if it were before me in a book. I raised my free hand and traced the same rune, adding my own light to his, sending spirals of color across the night's blank canvas. Our power surged together as it did before, wrapping around both of us and becoming stronger with the two of us feeding it. The crowd gasped as we both continued the show, culminating in a grand finale of riotous color and light, before we lowered our arms and let the magic fade.

When Raith looked into my eyes, my heart soared. We were both breathing fast, our faces flushed from exertion and the rush that came from doing magic together. Everything about it felt right, as if all our lives we'd been doing magic wrong because we hadn't been doing it together. But did he feel the same?

SEVENTEEN

ROSE

When I returned to my room after the grand feast in the temple, it was already well past midnight, though you couldn't tell based on the torchlight illuminating every inch of the castle. Raith and I hadn't been alone for even a second all evening, but I wouldn't be able to sleep until I knew the truth about the darkness everyone was so afraid of, no matter how exhausted I was after the long day. And unlike most other nights, Raith had retired to his bedroom, instead of disappearing into his study or teleporting somewhere else.

After Loura removed my gown and helped me prepare for bed, I dismissed her with a warm thanks. Once she was gone, I knocked on the connecting door to Raith's room. When he didn't answer, I banged harder, again and again, growing more and more annoyed at him for avoiding me. "I know you're in there!"

The door flew open. "What is it?"

He stood before me in nothing but black silk trousers, which hung low on his hips, and I was momentarily stunned into silence at the sight of all that naked skin in front of me. I'd seen him shirtless when he was sparring, but never this close. His chest was toned and lean, with a touch of dark hair trailing down his stomach and disappearing into his trousers. I swallowed hard, trying to remember why I'd wanted to speak with him, and noticed he seemed similarly entranced by the sight of me in my nearly see-through chemise. My nipples hardened at the knowledge he was looking at them with those intense gray eyes.

I tore my gaze away from his chest and crossed my arms. "Tell me about the darkness."

"Now?" He ran a hand over his weary face. "Can it not wait until tomorrow?"

"No, it cannot." I paused and tried a different tactic. "Please, Raith, I can't be a good queen if I don't know what is plaguing the kingdom."

"Very well. I suppose it's time you knew." He sighed and leaned against the doorway. "It started almost three years ago when living darkness began to take shape and spread across the land."

I stared at him, trying to make sense of his words. "Living darkness?"

"Thick, tangible shadows that creep over houses and farms to smother them, along with phantom beasts that attack people and animals. At first it only occurred in the eastern part of Ilidan, but over time it grew stronger and spread across the kingdom. Now it can swallow entire villages whole in one evening, unless I fight it back." Exhaustion crept into his voice, not just from tonight, but from years of battling this strange enemy. "Weapons are useless against them, as is water. Fire, light, and magic are the only ways to combat the shadows. Even then, we seem to be losing the battle."

I'd never heard of such terrible magic before. I had so many questions I didn't know where to begin, even as so many things began to fall into place. But my most pressing question was, "Why didn't you tell me?"

He looked away, crossing his arms. "It was none of your concern."

"Everything in Ilidan is my concern! Especially something this big. How many times must I say it?" I took a step closer, looking up at him with pleading eyes. "Do you not trust me? Surely by now you know I would never betray you or Ilidan by telling my father about this. Or anyone else, for that matter."

"Of course I trust you."

"Then why?" Another thought occurred to me. "Is this where you go every night? To fight the darkness on your own?"

One of his eyebrows shot up. "Why? Would you rather I spent those nights in your bed?"

"Don't change the subject," I said, even as desire flared at the picture he'd conjured in my head. "Is it?"

"Yes, that's where I go every night."

I nodded, relieved to finally know the truth. "Then let me go with you next time."

"No," he commanded. "Definitely not. The darkness is dangerous, and I want you nowhere near it."

"But I can help you! You said my magic is strong, and my fire affinity will work on the darkness. Maybe together we can stop the shadows from hurting anyone else."

His eyes narrowed. "I've spent the last few years doing everything I can to stop the Shadow Lord from taking over my kingdom. I've cast every rune I know to keep the darkness at bay. I've scoured the library for answers. I've asked other wizards for advice. If none of that has worked, what do you think *you* can do?"

I was so frustrated with him I could scream. All I wanted was to help him and the people of Ilidan, but he wouldn't let me. "I don't know, but there must be something. If we work together, we—"

"No," he said, his voice leaving little room for argument. "There is nothing you can do. In fact, I order you to stay out of it."

"You *order* me?" That was it. I raised my hand to trace a rune in the air, to show him I wasn't just some helpless princess but a wizard like he was, but he caught my wrist. As he held me, heat flared between us and his eyes dropped to my lips. The moment instantly changed, shifting from anger to desire, and the air practically crackled between us. Intense longing flooded me as I waited for him to kiss me, hoping he wanted me at least half as much as I wanted him. I nearly rose up on my toes to press my lips to his, but I needed him to do it first. I held my breath, waiting, waiting, waiting.

After an eternity, he took a sharp breath and dropped my hand. "I don't want you involved, Rose. I've already lost too much in my life. I can't lose you as well."

He closed the door in my face, stunning me with the vulnerability in his voice as much as his abrupt departure. Once again he'd rejected me, but he'd also implied he cared for me as well. That I meant something to him. Maybe there was hope for us after all.

But that didn't mean I was giving up on this.

EIGHTEEN

ROSE

I woke with a new sense of purpose and determination. I was going to find a way to save Ilidan from this threat, whatever it took. Raith obviously needed my help, even if he refused to admit it. He couldn't keep fighting the darkness on his own for much longer. It was already running him ragged, and even he admitted he was losing the battle. At least if I helped, he might be able to get some sleep now and then.

I marched toward his workshop, where I found him pouring something into a large flask. He traced a rune on the side of the glass and the liquid began to bubble, sending pale yellow smoke into the air.

"What is that?" I asked. "Something to help fight the shadows?"

He gave a soft snort. "Hardly. It's a potion to ease toothache. One of the kitchen staff asked me for it."

"That's kind of you." I leaned forward to examine it, but the smell of rotten egg made me cover my nose. I grabbed a stool and sat on it, smoothing out my skirts. "I want to know more about the darkness. What's causing the attacks? Where did it start? How often does it happen?"

He leveled his gaze at me and did not look amused. Not at all. "I told you I didn't want you involved in this matter."

"And I told you that Ilidan is my home now, and it's people are my responsibility too. It's clear you don't think I can help, but you won't know that until we try. I bring a fresh perspective to the matter."

"You bring trouble, is what you bring." He sighed and ran a hand over his face, looking exhausted again. My chest ached with the desire to comfort him or ease his troubles however I could. "As I said last night, it started almost three years ago on the eastern side of the kingdom. I'm not sure why or how, and the attacks have been increasing in frequency. They used to occur every few months. Then every few weeks. Now it's nearly every night."

"What is causing it?"

"No one knows, but I believe the Shadow Lord is sending the darkness. He's been spotted near some of the areas that have been attacked, though I've never encountered him myself. I'm sure it's only a matter of time though."

"The Shadow Lord," I said in nearly a whisper. He ruled another realm, the one wizards stepped inside to teleport, but little else was known about him. "Why would he do this?"

"I don't know. Perhaps he's upset because I have an

affinity for shadow. Perhaps I've done something to offend him. Perhaps he simply wants to take over this kingdom." He ran a hand through his black hair. "It doesn't matter. Whatever his motive, the attacks continue."

I remembered that huge shadowy profile I'd glimpsed from the window outside the castle. "I think I saw him once. On my first night here."

His face darkened. "He grows bolder every day. More reason for you to stay out of this."

"I'm not staying out of it. In fact, I want to go with you next time to fight the darkness."

"I already said no."

"Raith, look at you. You're so exhausted you can barely stand. You need my help."

His eyes narrowed. "Show me you can cast runes without using your hands, and then I'll consider it."

I blinked at him. "What?"

"My father never let me use my hands. He said that was for the weak. True wizards need not do such things." He tilted his head as he appraised me. "If you think you can fight the Shadow Lord's minions, you'll need to be able to cast spells quickly, faster than you can draw runes. Otherwise they will cut you down where you stand."

I swallowed. "I don't think I'm strong enough."

"You are. You're more powerful than you know."

His confidence in me was refreshing, but confusing. Did he want my help or not? Either way he was getting it, so I supposed I'd better try at least.

I concentrated on the fire rune, since that one was

nearly as easy for me to cast as breathing, but my fingers kept jumping up to trace the symbol in the air. I let out a frustrated sound and tried again, but couldn't do it.

"Let me help," Raith said.

He moved behind me, close enough to make my heart skip a beat, then took my hands in his own. He pulled my arms behind me as if holding me captive, his fingers circling my wrists, and the pose was so intimate it sent a rush of heat between my legs. "Cast the rune now."

I tugged against his grip lightly. "I can't."

"You can. I know you can." His mouth brushed against my hair. "Show me."

At first, I couldn't even conjure the rune in my mind, not with Raith touching me like this. All I could think about was how I wished his hands and mouth would go even further. Or how I could turn my head and brush my lips across his if I was brave enough. I wondered what he would do. Would he pull away? Or kiss me back even harder?

I drew in a breath and tried to focus. Thinking about Raith like that wouldn't help with fighting the darkness. I had to prove to him I was the wizard who could stand at his side against whatever we faced, and to do that, I needed to cast this spell. Yet every time I tried, my hand started to lift up to draw it, and Raith held me back. I let out a soft cry and tried to break free, but he restrained me tighter. Not enough to harm me, and I could certainly pull away if I truly wanted, but enough to make his point.

I remembered the other time he stood behind me, when he'd blindfolded me and practiced tracing the runes with me. His hands were on me then too. I closed my eyes as I envisioned it, the way we'd cast the spell together, how it had felt when both of our powers had mingled. With a gasp, the magic flowed out of me, and when I opened my eyes, I saw it—a glowing ball of fire hovering in front of us.

"It's a start," Raith said, as he released my wrists. "Now do it again."

Raith made me practice until supper time, and even then I didn't think he was truly satisfied. Casting the runes in my mind did not come naturally to me, and half the time I ended up using my hands out of habit, but I would keep trying. I would get better somehow. If there was one thing I possessed, it was sheer stubbornness.

As we sat down at the dining table, I slumped back in my seat, completely exhausted. "I suppose you won't let me help you anytime soon after that display."

"Don't be so hard on yourself. Most wizards can't cast runes with their minds at all. I'm surprised you got it so quickly, actually."

His rare praise made me pause. "You are?"

"It takes most wizards many years of training to even get close to that level, but you're a fast learner and you're determined." He lifted his spoon, but hesitated. "Perhaps all those years practicing on your own were not wasted after all."

I couldn't stop the smile bursting out of me. I wanted to jump on the table and do a little jig. I wanted to grab his face and press my mouth against his. "Maybe you can teach me to make potions next."

He let out a groan, but there was an amused look on his face as well. A slight twitch of his lips as if he might actually smile. I longed for that moment. Someday I'd get there. Someday he'd open up to me. Someday he wouldn't be able to resist.

Oren entered the room and bent over Raith to speak quietly with him. Raith's brow creased at whatever Oren said, before he nodded.

Raith rose to his feet. "I'm sorry Rose, but I must cut our supper short." He strode from the room before I could utter a word, while Oren cast me an apologetic look.

I threw my napkin on the table and ran after my husband, down the long hall toward his study. "Raith, wait! Where are you going?"

He spun toward me so fast I nearly ran into him. "I go to face the darkness, as I do every night."

"Let me come with you."

"No." He continued walking, his pace brisk.

I followed right at his heels. "You said I could help as long as I could cast spells without drawing the runes, and I can."

"Barely."

"Raith, please!" I caught his hand, pulling him back toward me. "Let me help you!"

He towered over me, but instead of pushing me away, he took my face in his hands and stared into my eyes. "Rose, you are the one thing in the world I still hold dear. I will not risk losing you too."

His mouth landed on mine, capturing anything I might

have said in reply. He tasted like red wine and stormy nights and every secret I'd always wanted to uncover. I'd been kissed before, but never with such intense passion, and never with a yearning so strong I thought it might burn me up from the inside. His long fingers slid into my hair, pulling me closer, his lips moving with mine in an intimate dance I never wanted to end.

But then he released me with a tortured groan and took a step back. All I could do was stand there, completely stunned by his words and his kiss, while he vanished before my eyes. I touched my lips, my heart aching anew knowing he would be out there fighting the shadows on his own—and there was nothing I could do to help him.

Not yet anyway.

NINETEEN

RAITH

When I opened my eyes, all I saw was darkness. The smell of damp grass tickled my nose from where my face was pressed against the cold ground. My entire body ached, and I groaned as I pushed myself up on my arms and tried to figure out where I was.

The moon was hidden tonight behind thick clouds. I cast a quick light spell, but the illumination did little to answer my questions. I was in the middle of the forest with nothing around me but trees and dirt as far as I could see. How had I gotten here?

I rose to my feet and stumbled a little, my head bursting with pain and weariness. I pressed a hand to my temple as I dragged up the memories from the depths of my mind. Kissing Rose. Teleporting to the village. Fighting back the darkness encasing it. And then...nothing.

I must have tried to teleport back to Varlock Castle and

ended up here somehow before passing out from exhaustion. Normally I made it back to my study before that happened, but tonight had been especially taxing. The darkness had returned to Haversham and I'd barely been able to expel it. Next time I wasn't sure I'd be successful.

I glanced up at the dark sky, trying to gauge the time. How long had I been lying here in the middle of nowhere? Was Rose waiting up for me?

Why in the world had I kissed her?

I sucked in a breath to steel myself, then gathered the shadows to teleport to my study. As the darkness receded, I spotted her on the chaise lounge, but this time her nose was in a book, though her eyes were half-closed.

"Raith!" she cried, as she jumped to her feet.

I took an unsteady step toward her and she threw herself at me, knocking the air from my lungs. She buried her face against my chest, her fingers gripping my shirt, and I wrapped my arms around her and held her tight against me. I pressed my face into her dark hair and closed my eyes, breathing her in while savoring the feel of her soft curves against my body. It had been so long since I'd held a woman in my arms like his. I knew I should pull away, to stop this before it went any further, but I couldn't. I told myself it was exhaustion and nothing more, but that was a lie.

Finally, she looked up at me. "I was so worried. You were gone so long."

I stared at her lips, those lush, beautiful lips I'd tasted only hours earlier. It had been foolish to kiss her before. It would be doubly foolish to kiss her again now. But Sun and Moon, how I wanted to.

I forced myself to pull away from her. "I'm fine."

"Tell me what happened."

I pinched the bridge of my nose, trying to fight off my pounding headache. "The darkness was stronger than ever before. I could barely hold it back. But I did."

"And now you're exhausted again." She stepped toward me, her eyes burning with determination. "This is why you need my help."

"No," I repeated for what felt like the hundredth time.

She opened her mouth as if to argue, but then stopped and took my hand instead. "Come with me."

With her fingers clasped tight around mine, she dragged me out of the study. I stumbled after her, trying not to show how weary I was.

"Where are you taking me?" I asked.

"To bed."

My eyebrows darted up at that very alluring thought. "I suspect I won't have much stamina right now, my dear wife."

She gave me a sharp look. "Not for that. You need to sleep. You'll be useless to everyone if you pass out in the middle of your study, and I need you to teach me more spells tomorrow."

"Is that all you want me for?" I asked, my exhaustion making me loose with my tongue.

"Tomorrow? Yes. Tomorrow night... We'll see." She gave me a smoldering look that made me instantly hard, before shoving open the door to my chambers. She led me through the sitting room and into the bedroom, where she cast a spell that instantly lit all the candles inside, without using her hands at all. Sun and Moon, she'd learned to do that quickly. It had taken me months, much to my father's dismay. If Rose had been trained from childhood as I was, she might even rival the Archwizard in power.

"We should get you out of those damp clothes," she said. "You look like you went rolling in the gardens."

Not far off, I thought, as I unclasped my cloak. She took it from me and draped it near the newly-lit hearth, while I kicked off my shoes. "I could dry these clothes myself," I muttered.

She snorted. "You're not fit to cast any spells, and I don't know the rune for that one. We'll have to dry your clothes the old-fashioned way. Now get them off."

This had gone far enough. I was definitely not taking my clothes off in front of her. And if she stayed in my bedroom much longer, I wasn't sure I could resist taking hers off, no matter how tired I was.

I moved to the connecting door and threw it open. "It's time for you to return to your room. You need some sleep as well."

Her brow furrowed, but she didn't budge. "Are you sure you're all right?"

"Perfectly fine," I said, standing a little taller.

"Very well," she said, her voice doubtful. "But there's something I should tell you."

"What is it?"

She glanced at the covered window with a frown. "I saw the Shadow Lord again."

"Where?" I asked, striding toward her. "When?"

"While you were gone. I spotted him through your study window." She wrapped her arms around herself like she was suppressing a chill. "He was closer than before."

I couldn't help myself—I pulled her into my arms, both worried for her safety and relieved nothing had happened. "What did he look like? What was he doing?"

"He was skulking through the gardens. He looked like a giant man made of living darkness with massive wings. As I watched, he took to the air and flew away." She shuddered, and I tightened my hold on her.

"I'll stop him," I said. "I'll find a way."

"I know you will. I believe in you. I simply want to help however I can."

I sighed and pressed my forehead against hers. "Right now, you can help me by staying safe inside the castle. And getting some sleep."

Her hand cupped my cheek, her touch so tender it made me lean into it. "Sleep I can do. But I'll never give up on trying to help you. I'm your queen and your wife. I want to be your partner too."

With that, she pressed a quick kiss to my lips before leaving the room. As the door shut, I could only stare after her, while longing tore me apart in ways the darkness never would.

TWENTY

I smoothed my gloved hands down the front of my emerald green dress before checking my crown one last time, along with the former Queen's jewels, which hung around my neck. Everything was in place and I'd always enjoyed balls, so why was I so nervous?

A man with a deep, bellowing voice announced, "Her Majesty, Queen Rose."

The double doors flew open in front of me. I sucked in a breath and stepped through them into the ballroom while my long gown flowed behind me. The entire room seemed to pause and turn toward me, and my heart raced knowing hundreds of eyes were appraising me and taking stock of their former enemy and new queen.

I searched the crowd, but I didn't recognize anyone in front of me until my eyes landed on Raith across the room. His tall, dark profile immediately drew me toward him, as did his commanding presence. Even in the middle of a crowd he was the only one I saw. It had been two days since I'd helped him to his room, and I was certain he'd been avoiding me all that time, though he did attend our nightly meals, at least for a few minutes.

A man moved in front of me, blocking my view of my husband. A very handsome man, and from the arrogant smile on his face, he knew it. His dark brown hair was perfectly tousled with one curl hanging over his blue eyes. His broad shoulders filled out his maroon coat and tapered down to a narrow waist. Everything about him was confident and screamed of wealth and privilege.

"Your majesty, you're even more beautiful than I'd heard." He swept into a deep, graceful bow. "Allow me to introduce myself. I am Lord Malren, Raith's cousin."

Malren. I stood a little straighter at the name. Raith had warned me about him. "It's a pleasure to meet you."

"The pleasure is all mine." He flashed me a dazzling smile. "Might I have this dance?"

I glanced around us, but Raith was caught up in conversation with another nobleman and no one else was coming to my rescue. I didn't trust Malren, but I couldn't refuse him a dance. We were family now, after all. Not to mention he was next in line for the throne and a powerful nobleman in his own right. I doubted Raith would dance with me anyway.

"That would be lovely," I said, as I offered Malren my gloved hand.

He took it and swept me forward onto the dance floor,

while people parted for us. His firm fingers clasped mine, while his other hand rested on my waist. The next song began, and we moved together in time to the music, our movements fluid and graceful.

"You're a fine dancer," Malren said. "Was dancing a pastime of yours in Talador?"

"We have our fair share of balls, yes."

"I'm sure you were the belle of all of them."

I laughed. "Hardly. I have five beautiful sisters, after all."

"So I've heard, though I doubt any can compare to the woman in front of me now." He gave me another charming smile. "How are you adjusting to life in Ilidan?"

"I like it so far, though I sometimes miss my home. I'm hoping I can visit my family again soon."

"Of course. It's natural for you to be homesick after leaving behind your old life so suddenly." His hand slid from my waist to my lower back, pulling me closer against him. "Did you know your father and I are allies?"

My eyebrows darted up. "No, I was not aware."

"We've negotiated some deals before, even during the war. Now that trade has resumed between the two kingdoms, I believe he and I can become even better allies."

Something in his tone sent a chill up my spine. "I'm sure he would be interested in that."

"I'm glad you think so." His eyes studied my face and he smiled again. "In fact, there's something I'd like to get your opinion on."

"Is that so?" I tried to keep my voice friendly, even

though everything he said made me more and more suspicious.

"It's no secret that our king is failing Ilidan. He's tried his best to save this kingdom and made great progress when he married you, no doubt. But the Shadow Lord is taking over our land and Raith cannot stop it. The area around my holdings has been either abandoned, decimated, or taken by the darkness. We're barely hanging on at this point."

"I'm sorry to hear that," I said, and I truly was. "I hadn't realized it had gotten so bad."

"It gets worse every night. I shouldn't even be here." He shook his head, but I couldn't tell if the sadness in his voice was genuine or not. "It's become clear to me that the Shadow Lord has some vendetta against Raith, and he won't stop until our king is dead."

"And you're second in line for the throne." I tried to seem intrigued, while hiding the true horror I felt at his words.

"That's true, although I assure you, I am only concerned about Ilidan's future, not about winning the throne." Sun and Moon, he almost sounded sincere. His head lowered, his lips brushing against the hair near my ear. "But if something were to happen to Raith, I would welcome you as my queen. Gladly."

"That is reassuring." I gave him what I hoped was an alluring smile. I had to keep him talking to find out more about his intentions, even if I could hardly stand another minute dancing in his arms. "I'm definitely intrigued. Do you have something planned already? And is my father helping you with this?"

"Not yet, but let's just say it isn't the first time we've taken out one of the royal family." He gave me a slight nod, his eyes gleaming. "I think you know what I mean."

I gasped, freezing in the middle of our dance. "The princess?"

"As I said, your father and I have worked together in the past with some success. I'd love it if you and I could be allies as well." He gave me a cocky smile as his hand moved down the back of my dress, smoothing over my behind. "Or even more."

Disgust burned inside me, and it took every ounce of my self-control not to pull away. Somehow I had to pretend to go along with this so I could learn more, but the thought made me sick. He was the reason Raith's first wife was dead, and now he wanted to get rid of my husband too. How could he ever think I'd agree to that?

Before I could reply, Raith appeared beside us and rested his hand on my arm. "Mind if I dance with my wife?" he asked, making every word sound like a dagger.

"Of course, cousin." Malren gave him a sharp smile. "Although it's a shame I can't keep her for myself."

Raith's eyes narrowed. "I'm sure there are plenty of other ladies who'd be delighted to dance with you."

"Ah, but none are as lovely as Queen Rose. We'll speak again soon, I'm sure." He slowly released me and flashed me a wink, before slipping into the crowd.

As soon as his cousin was gone, Raith clasped my hand

tightly, yanking me against his chest. "What was that about?" he snapped.

I rested my hand on Raith's shoulder and met his eyes, oddly pleased at his show of possessiveness. It had gotten him to dance with me, at least. "Your cousin asked me to dance. Should I have refused him?"

Raith's fingers tightened on my waist in a way that made heat rush between my thighs. "I didn't like the way he was looking at you. And he seemed to be holding you a bit closer than necessary."

A soft laugh escaped me. "My dear husband, are you jealous?"

He whisked me across the dance floor with a frown. "Hardly. I simply don't trust him."

"Then trust me," I said, sliding my hand to his neck. "You have nothing to be jealous of, I promise." I brought my lips close to his ear and whispered. "Malren seems to think I might be a potential ally. I was trying to get as much information as possible about his schemes so that we could stop him."

His fingers relaxed a little, but he still held me close. "What did you uncover?"

"Nothing I can discuss in the middle of a ball." If I told Raith that Malren might have been involved in his wife's murder, I could only imagine what he would do. Better to tell him when Malren was out of the castle and Raith could rage in private. "I'll try to get more out of him throughout the evening. In fact, it'd be better if we split up for the rest of the night."

"After this song," Raith said, as he spun me around with expert grace. Every eye in the room followed us, the other nobles watching us intently with expressions ranging from curiosity to disapproval. I knew Raith might be dancing with me just to appease them, but I didn't think so. Not from the way he held me against his chest, like he wanted every man in the room to know I was *his*.

"So you do like dancing," I said, unable to hide my smile. I was finally getting the dance I'd wanted during our wedding feast.

"With the right woman," he grudgingly admitted. "It's been many years since I've done it though."

"I'm honored. You're quite good at it, as well. Better than I expected."

His jaw clenched. "Just because I choose not to dance doesn't mean I don't know how."

The song finished and we slowly stepped back and bowed to each other, though I was sad to break away from Raith's embrace. I longed to spend the entire night in his arms, preferably without all of our guests watching us. From the way his eyes smoldered at me, I thought he might want the same thing.

Eventually I remembered the others in the room. "You should introduce me to some of our guests."

"I will, but first I have a surprise for you."

I tilted my head. "A surprise?"

"Come." He looped his arm through mine and led me across the ballroom, while the guests made no attempt to hide their stares. Good, let them see that the two of us were united. My back straightened as the crowd parted for us, and I tried to look as regal as possible at Raith's side. But when I saw the surprise, I couldn't help but gasp. Standing alongside a tall column was someone I never expected to see.

"Lily?" I cried out as I grabbed my skirts and rushed forward, forgetting everyone else at the ball.

My older sister turned her serene face toward me, and her smile made my heart leap. She wore a pale blue gown that looked like frost, along with her icicle tiara, and it was so good to see her I thought my chest might burst with happiness. I flung myself into her arms, while she hugged me back and laughed softly, remaining composed as always.

"What are you doing here?" I asked.

"Your husband was kind enough to invite me and provided transportation for both of us," she said, gesturing to the handsome guard beside her. Captain Keane never left her side, so it didn't surprise me that he'd insisted on coming with her. He gave me a quick nod while his dark blue eyes scanned the room for threats.

I spun around to face Raith. "You teleported them here?"

Raith watched our reunion with an expression I couldn't read. "I did."

Warmth spread through me at his kind gesture, and emotion made my eyes tear up a little. "Thank you."

He cleared his throat and looked away. "I thought it would be a good gesture to show the people that Ilidan and Talator truly are at peace."

"Of course," I said, though I suspected he'd really done it for me. He knew how much I missed my sisters, and even though I wrote to them frequently, it was still not the same as seeing them every day of my life. I lifted on my toes to press a kiss to his cheek, and he looked at me with surprise after my lips brushed against his skin.

I took Lily's hand and led her to a bench in the corner of the ballroom, while Keane trailed behind us. "Come, we have so much to catch up on. I want to hear about every-thing that's happening back at Winton Castle. How are our sisters? Aunt Dahlia? Father?"

She shook her head with amusement, a faint smile on her lips. "Everyone is well, although we miss you, naturally. It's dreadfully cold at the castle already, but we manage as we always do. But I want to hear all about your life here. How are you settling in? Is King Raith treating you well?"

"Yes, he is. He's been teaching me magic." I traced a rune in the air and a snowflake appeared in front of Lily's face. She looked at it hesitantly, before taking it into her hand.

"Incredible," she said, as it slowed crumbled in her fingers and then vanished.

"My affinity is for fire actually, which would have been useful back in Talador if I'd known. I've been practicing magic almost every day, and Raith says I'm learning quickly."

She rested her hand over mine. "Perhaps the Sun and Moon truly brought the two of you together for a reason. Now you can learn all the things you always wanted to know." She glanced behind me, where Raith was talking to Oren. "But are you happy?"

"I'm...as happy as can be expected, I suppose. I miss all of you so much, but I do like my new life here, surprisingly. I have purpose and responsibility that I never had back in Talador. Raith and I respect one another. We've become...friends."

"Is that all? Friends?" She arched an eyebrow. "I saw the two of you dancing together. The way he looked at you... there must be something more there."

Heat rushed to my cheeks, and I couldn't help but follow her gaze to Raith's back. "I don't know. Maybe. I hope so."

"You care for him."

I let out a breath. "Yes, very much."

"He cares for you as well." Lily had always been good at reading people, a useful skill when one was a future queen.

"I suppose he does, in his way, but he's still not over his previous wife, whom he loved very much. I cannot blame him for still grieving her. Not to mention, the..." My words trailed off as I realized I was about to tell Lily about the darkness, but I stopped myself. I'd promised Raith I wouldn't tell anyone about it, and that included my sister. For the first time ever, she and I had different allegiances. She would always be bound to Talador, while my duty was to Ilidan now.

"The what?" she asked.

"The circumstances surrounding our marriage," I said quickly. "Raith and I were both forced into this alliance, but we've made the best of it. It's a miracle he can even look at me at all after what our father did." I bowed my head and whispered, "Father was the one responsible for Raith's wife's death."

Lily raised a hand to her mouth, her face horrified. "Are you certain?"

"Not entirely, but it sounds like he sent assassins to take out Raith and his wife when they were traveling to her parents' estate. Raith was delayed, but they still took her life. I believe Lord Malren, Raith's cousin, was working with our father to set it up, but I have no proof. Do you think you could look for something when you return home?"

Her brow furrowed. "I can try. I'm truly sorry, Rose. I had no idea Father was involved in such a thing."

"Me neither, though it doesn't surprise me." I squeezed her hand. "Someday you will be Queen and we can right all of these wrongs and end the legacy of bloodshed in our lands."

She leaned against me as we watched the other guests dance. "I pray you are right. Father is pushing me to choose a husband again."

To the side, Keane tensed up slightly. It was barely noticeable, but I could tell every muscle in his body had stiffened at her words. I'd always suspected he had feelings for my sister, though he would never act on them and she was oblivious. A shame, really. Keane might be the only man I trusted with my sister's heart.

TWENTY-ONE

RAITH

I left Rose and her sister to catch up, while I moved through the crowd and greeted my guests. Though I'd never been a fan of large events or balls, this one seemed to drag on more than normal. I found myself longing for a quiet dinner alone with my wife where she chatted my ear off about her life before we met. I nearly smiled as I thought of her last story, about how she and Jasmine had pranked Lily when they were younger by locking a squirrel in the older sister's wardrobe. They'd only meant to startle Lily, excited to see the look on her normally stoic face, but the animal chewed a hole in the wood and escaped, then caused havoc all over her bedroom. Needless to say, King Balsam had not been amused.

It would do Rose some good to see her sister again, even if only for a few hours, but that wasn't the only reason I'd brought Lily tonight. Many of the nobles here were curious about both of the women and wished to speak with them. Hopefully it would ease some of the tensions between our two nations if people saw that both sides were behaving and being civil.

Although some people were decidedly *not* behaving. I caught sight of Lord Malren and remembered the way he'd held my wife intimately, his hand sliding down to her behind. I'd nearly struck him with lightning at the sight of him touching her there. Now he stood with three other women fawning all over him, though they scattered like mice as I approached.

"Stay away from my wife, Malren," I growled.

My cousin flashed me a smile that he probably thought made him look charming, but I only saw a snake. "Come now, Raith, I was simply getting to know her. She is family, after all." His smile turned predatory. "Besides, if the rumors are true, you've not yet taken her to bed. She must be terribly lonely. I'd be happy to keep her company."

My eyes narrowed and I nearly struck him across the face for his words. I wanted nothing more than to send him into the Shadow Lands, but there were too many people watching this exchange. I took a step closer, lacing my voice with threat. "Don't even think about it."

"Her sister is quite beautiful too, and I heard she's in need of a husband." He glanced over at the two of them. "King of Talador has a nice right to it, don't you think? I'd prefer Ilidan, but I'm not picky."

My fists clenched at my side. "As soon as the sun rises, I want you gone from this castle."

I spun on my heel to walk away, but Malren's laugh echoed behind me. "Your time on the throne is limited, cousin. The darkness won't stop until you're dead. The entire kingdom knows it. Surely you can see it too?"

Fury made lightning crackle on my fingertips and shadows animate at my side, but I kept walking. Malren must have eyes and ears inside the castle to know so much about my personal relations with Rose. Not that I would expect any less of him, but it was a good reminder to be careful.

It was bad enough he'd threatened my throne, but then he'd dare to bring up my relationship with Rose. I may not have taken her to bed yet, but she was *mine*. I was tempted to remedy the problem immediately, but Rose was still with her sister and I would not interrupt their time together.

An older woman with white-streaked blond hair approached me, wearing a distractingly large brooch of a bumblebee on her violet dress. She dipped into a slight curtsey before me, her movements stiff. "Congratulations on your marriage, King Raith."

"Thank you, Lady Joyena." I bowed my head to her. She was Silena's grandmother and had always been kind to me, if a bit eccentric. I offered her my arm, and she took it as we strolled around the edge of the ballroom together. "I'm pleased you could join us tonight."

"I wouldn't miss it. I never thought the war would end in my lifetime." She patted my hand with her wrinkled fingers. "Your parents would be proud. My only question is, can your new wife be trusted?"

"I believe so. She wants peace as much as we do."

"I've heard rumors she is a wizard as well. Is that so?"

"Yes, and quite powerful too."

She offered me a kind smile. "Then I pray to the Sun and Moon for many healthy children, and that she can help put an end to the dark plague spreading across the land."

I couldn't think about either of those things without my chest tightening. "We're doing everything we can to stop it together."

"Very good." She turned toward me, her eyes softening. "Silena would also be proud of you, you know."

My throat closed up, and I grasped the ring on the chain around my neck. "I think of her every day."

"Me too. Such a sweet girl, and taken from us way too young. But she would want you to be happy. Never forget that."

With a nod and a warm smile, she walked away, leaving me with only my thoughts and memories. If Silena would want me to be happy, why did I feel like I was betraying her every time I looked at Rose?

TWENTY-TWO

ROSE

Lily and I spent the rest of the evening talking to various nobles from across Ilidan, giving assurances that the war was truly over with Talador and that both kingdoms were devoted to peace. Many of them wished to discuss trade with Lily, which seemed like a good sign. I never got a chance to speak to Lord Malren alone again, as he was often surrounded by at least three women hanging onto his every word, though I caught him sending many glances my way.

When the hour grew late, Lily said her goodbyes before Raith teleported her and Keane back to Talador. By then, my feet were sore, and I was feeling a bit suffocated by all the people hovering around me. I managed to escape past a guard who warned me not to go outside, and I stepped onto the balcony overlooking the garden. Cool night air wrapped around me and I breathed it in, along with the silence. I didn't mind strangers and had never been shy, but being a queen was very different from being one of six princesses, and the least favorite one to boot. Suddenly people asked my opinion on just about everything or wanted my help, and the responsibility was overwhelming. How did Raith handle it every day?

As if my thoughts had summoned him, he stepped outside onto the balcony. "You shouldn't be out here, Rose."

I rolled my eyes as I turned toward him. "We're perfectly safe. There is enough light to make the sun jealous."

"You spotted the Shadow Lord the other night in this very garden."

"Good, maybe he'll return. I have a few words for him."

Raith gave an exasperated sigh. "Your father did warn me you were a handful."

I gave him a wry smile. "Wishing you'd chosen one of my sisters now?"

His hands slid around my waist, making my pulse race. "Not even a little."

He brought his lips to mine and I wrapped my arms around his neck, fitting my body against his. His kiss was possessive and seductive, desperate and intense, like he wanted to prove I was his and only his, even though I'd never wanted to be anyone else's.

"I've wanted to do that all evening," he said against my lips.

"Me too."

He kissed me harder, his tongue sliding against mine in

a way that made me wonder what else he could do with it. Between our dance earlier and his surprise invitation of Lily, I knew Raith cared for me more than he would ever admit. And from the way he kissed, I was starting to think he desired me as much as I desired him too.

"Come to my room tonight," I said, between breaths quickened with desire. "Please."

"Rose... I can't." His thumbs slid across my lower lip, which was still wet with the taste of him. His face turned away. "I shouldn't even be kissing you."

"Why not?" I asked, as he slipped from my hands and put distance between us. "We're married. It seems like you have feelings for me, and I care for you too."

He met my eyes with an intense smolder. "That's the problem. I don't want to feel anything."

He headed into the castle, though not before stopping to cast a spell that made all the torches flare bright around me. Another sign he cared, even if he refused to admit it. I sighed as he slipped back into the crowd and began speaking with some of the nobles.

No matter how distant Raith was, and no matter how much he pushed me away, I couldn't resist being drawn to him. It was foolish of me to hope for anything more between us, but I couldn't help myself. As I watched him speak to the nobles while radiating confidence and power, I knew why. It was more than his magnetic presence, it was his devotion to his people. He loved his kingdom more than anything, and he would do whatever it took to protect them. Including marrying the daughter of the man who had killed his wife.

Or going out every night to fight the darkness, even to the point of exhaustion.

There was something undeniably sexy about a king who would put his people above his own happiness. No matter how much Raith played the cold, brooding wizard, his heart was larger than he knew.

I only wished he would let me into it.

TWENTY-THREE

ROSE

The ball lasted all throughout the evening and until dawn, since no one would travel while it was dark. Many danced away the entire night, while others retired to guest rooms for the evening, including Lord Malren, who had the nerve to send a note inviting me to his bed. I wrote back claiming I was exhausted from the ball, but that I'd like to continue our discussion another time. Hopefully that would give him the idea I was willing to be allies so I could learn more of what he planned.

I truly was exhausted from entertaining people until the wee hours of the morning, and by the time I woke, it was late afternoon and all of our guests had left the castle already. As sunset fell, things returned to normal in the place I now thought of as my home. It was strange to think that only weeks ago this kingdom had been my enemy, or at best a strange land I could barely fathom. Now I couldn't imagine living anywhere else. Or with anyone else.

I gazed across the dining table at Raith during our evening meal. "Lord Malren invited me to his room last night."

Raith slammed his wine glass down. "What?"

"I said no, obviously." I took a sip from my own wine glass. "Although it's too bad I couldn't get more information out of him before he left."

Raith's eyes narrowed. "I don't want him near you."

"You don't need to worry. I can handle myself with Malren. If he tries anything, I can always set him on fire." But then my tone turned serious and I glanced down. "Although once you learn what he told me, you'll wish I had done exactly that."

"What is it?"

I was hesitant to tell him what I'd learned because it would bring him pain, but perhaps it could bring him some closure too, with the possibility of justice someday. But opening up old wounds was never easy. "Malren told me that he and my father have been allies for some time. He implied that he was in on my father's plan to assassinate you that resulted in your wife's death."

Raith's hand tightened around his fork. "He told you this?"

"Not outright, but the meaning was clear. I believe he helped my father, though I don't know how exactly."

Raith's face darkened as he slipped into a memory. "Silena and I were meant to visit her parents, who live in the estate next to Malren's holdings. I was delayed by some business in the castle, but told her I would catch up to her carriage later. Malren must have heard we were going to be traveling to her parents' that day, and then supplied that information to your father. The assassins simply had to wait off the road, knowing the carriage would pass by that exact spot on that day."

"I'm so sorry, Raith."

He shoved his food back and rose to his feet with a growl, his eyes blazing with cold fury. "I'm going to murder him. You should have told me before he left the castle." He grabbed his long black cloak and set it on his shoulders. "No matter. I can find him."

I jumped to my feet and rushed over before he did something rash. "This is exactly why I didn't tell you last night." I grabbed his arm tightly before he could teleport away, forcing him to look at me. "There's nothing you can do about Malren now. We need proof and all we have is speculation."

He stared down at me while menacing shadows shifted around him, coming to life with his rage. "I'm the King. I don't need proof."

"Please, Raith. Let me try to get more information out of him and figure out what he is planning." I swallowed. "Especially because he hinted he had something similar in the works for you, and that if I was willing to help he would take me as his queen."

"He will never have you or my throne!" Raith's face flashed with dangerous intent while his hands clenched into fists. A cruel smile curved across his sensual lips. "But I'd very much like to see him try to take them."

I slid my arms around his chest, wrapping him in a warm embrace. "We'll get proof of his involvement, and we'll make sure he is brought to justice, I promise. But at the moment there is nothing we can do, and we have more pressing problems."

I thought he would push me away and storm off, but after a moment he let out a long breath and his shoulders relaxed. His hands slid up my back and he drew me closer, resting his forehead against mine.

"Why are you helping me with this?" he asked.

"Partly because it's a way to atone for my father's sins." I stroked his neck softly with my fingertips, wondering how he could even ask me that. Wasn't it obvious how I felt? "But mostly because I care about you."

"It would be better if you didn't. All I bring is death and darkness to those close to me. If you know what's best for you, you'll stay far away."

"Lucky for you I don't care what's best for me."

I kissed him with my hand on his jaw, stroking the rough stubble there. He pulled me closer as he returned the kiss with vigor, like he couldn't help himself despite all his previous protests. He held me there as he took control of my mouth and body, his hands roaming across my dress. When he brushed the side of my breasts, I gasped into his lips, my fingers tightening on his shirt. As his tongue teased mine, his hand cupped one breast through the fabric, tracing the spot where my nipple had already hardened.

He was hard too. I could feel it even through all our layers of clothing, and it made me press closer against him, aching for more of his touch. Maybe he would stay tonight. Maybe he would choose me.

But then he groaned and tore his mouth away. "I can't do this, Rose." He glanced at the wooden clock on the wall. "And it's time for me to go. I received a report earlier that another town is in trouble."

"Don't leave," I begged, overcome with both worry and desire. "Stay with me tonight."

"I took last night off for the ball. I can't ignore my duty for a second time. The darkness grows stronger every minute I wait."

"Then take me with you!"

"You're not ready. I'll only be distracted and worried if you're by my side." He pressed one last kiss to my lips, before the shadows swallowed him up. He vanished in front of my eyes, leaving behind only a lingering wisp of darkness where he'd once stood.

I wanted to stomp my foot in frustration or howl at how unfair all of this was. Raith wouldn't admit it, but he couldn't keep fighting the darkness on his own. He'd barely made it back to the castle the other night. He said he was worried about me, but what of *my* worries? I couldn't lose Raith either.

With stubborn concern guiding my steps, I found Oren in the hallway outside the kitchens. "Where did he go tonight?"

Oren's face betrayed nothing. He was too well trained for that. "I can't say, my queen. I do apologize."

"Did he order you not to tell me?" I asked. When Oren didn't answer, I huffed but stood my ground. "Raith foolishly thinks he has to do everything on his own, but you and I both know he's wearing himself out and can't keep doing this much longer. One night he isn't going to return, and the darkness will win. But not if I'm there to help him."

"Maybe so, but he wouldn't want to risk your life, no matter what happens to him."

"This kingdom needs Raith alive." My heart clenched at the thought of losing him. "*I* need him alive."

Oren frowned, but I could tell I'd won him over. After a long pause, he said, "He went to Bellsover."

Relief flooded me. "How far is that?"

"Nearly a day's ride away."

My relief vanished. I had no idea where Bellsover was and no way to get there in time to help him.

Unless I could teleport like Raith.

"Thank you, Oren," I called out as I rushed down the hall. I raced through the castle with my skirts in hand, past curious servants and guards, before making it to Raith's workshop. I traced the rune to open the door and stepped inside, easily lighting all the candles at once with barely a thought.

There had to be a book in here that taught the teleportation spell. It wasn't in the one he'd given me, so I had to look for something more obscure. Something he wouldn't want me to read.

I quickly searched the tall bookshelves, pulling out various spell books and skimming through them, until I discovered one that was made of worn black leather entitled *Spells of Darkness and Shadow*. This had to be it.

I flipped past the warning on the opening page about how these spells were dangerous because they created a link to the Shadow Lands and began reading. Most of the spells were of little use to me, or sounded far too dangerous to try, but about halfway through I found what I was searching for.

The teleportation spell involved stepping into the Shadow Lands—where time and distance were different from our world—and then emerging in another place. To do it you had to imagine the place you wished to journey to while summoning the darkness with a complicated rune. The book warned that few wizards could manage such a thing, but I wasn't concerned.

One problem remained—I had never been to Bellsover. I had no clue what it looked like and only a vague sense of where it was, so there was no way I could conjure it in my head. But I'd come this far, and I wasn't giving up now.

I practiced tracing the complicated rune with my finger many times without magic before feeling confident I could cast the spell without error. I moved to the center of the room, took a deep breath, and then closed my eyes and thought of Raith. He was the location I wanted to travel to, no matter where he was. I imagined his brooding face, his raven black hair, and his commanding presence. I thought of the way he looked at me, as if he wanted me but hated himself for it. I replayed the sound of his voice when he said my name. And then I traced the rune and pushed power into it.

Darkness swept over me like a blanket tossed over my head and I nearly screamed, even though I'd done this once before. Back then I'd been with Raith, and although we'd only met hours before, I'd already been comforted beside him. Now I was alone in the Shadow Lands and had no idea what I was doing. And if I didn't get out fast, I could be trapped here forever.

I pictured Raith again, remembering the feel of his mouth on mine and the way he'd fondled my breast earlier. The darkness slipped away like water dripping down my body, until I was no longer in the workshop, but outside in the middle of an unfamiliar road on the edge of a town.

Or what used to be a town.

TWENTY-FOUR

ROSE

A chill ran down my spine at the sight of the town being swallowed up by shadows. I could make out the shapes of buildings and houses, but they were enveloped in a thick darkness that seemed to suck in all light around it. The inky thing covering the entire area was blacker than anything I'd ever seen before. Even the night sky on a moonless night was bright in comparison.

The darkness had a presence too, one I couldn't explain or deny. As I stared at it, I got the sense it was staring back at me. Watching me as I watched it. I stepped back involuntarily and swallowed the fear in my throat. This was what Raith fought night after night. It was a wonder he'd kept his sanity this long.

But there was beauty in the darkness too. Shadowy wisps curled and danced through the air as if reaching for something, while thicker patches of black gloom gleamed like fresh ink under the moonlight. The darkness called to me in a way I couldn't deny, whispering of hidden knowledge and dark secrets I might uncover if I was only brave enough to step into the abyss.

My husband's voice rang out in a sharp cry and jerked me out of my thoughts, drawing my attention to the other side of town.

"Raith!" I sprinted forward as best I could in my long black gown and slippers. The darkness shot out a shadowy tendril and tried to catch my leg, but I managed to narrowly avoid it. Fear boosted my speed as I headed through the nightmare, but the dark shapes confused my vision. The buildings were so black it was hard to tell how big they were or how far away. I called forth a ball of light beside me, but the surrounding darkness nearly absorbed it right up.

I spotted Raith standing in the middle of the cobblestone road, throwing lightning bolts at shadowy beasts that looked like no animals I'd seen before yet had borrowed parts from many of them. A claw here, a tail there, and some even had giant bat wings. They sprang up from the darkest corners around him and battered him relentlessly, but he fought them off with nothing but his magic and resolve.

There were too many. Soon he would go down—unless I helped him.

I drew runes in my mind as he'd taught me, summoning lances of fire that turned the black monsters to ash. They screeched and howled as they burnt up into the night, and I drew closer, letting my need to protect Raith overcome my fear of the beasts. I burned them all down with a vehemence

I didn't know I possessed. This was my kingdom now too, and these creatures did not belong in it—and they would not touch my husband.

As the last of the monsters turned to smoke, Raith turned looked my way and froze, like he couldn't believe his eyes. "Rose? What are you doing here?"

"Making sure Ilidan still has a King tomorrow."

He stormed over to me. "Are you mad? You shouldn't be here. It's too dangerous. How did you even get here?"

"I taught myself teleportation," I said, with a casual shrug.

"You did what?" He gaped at me. "Of all the foolish, dangerous, reckless things—"

I cut him off by pressing my lips against his in a desperate kiss full of urgency and relief. His hands gripped my upper arms and he let out a low groan as he kissed me back with the same passion.

But then he pulled away and his face was hard again. "You need to get back to the castle immediately. That was only the first wave of shadow beasts."

"I'm not leaving without you."

"You must." He ran a hand through his black hair, exhaustion coating his features. "I have to send the darkness back, but I've never seen it this strong before. If you stay, you'll only be in the way. I insist you return to the castle, Rose."

I glanced around at what was left of the town, but it was little more than a black void around us. "Come with me. There's nothing you can do here."

"I can't abandon Bellsover."

My voice softened. "Raith, it's already gone."

He turned away from me, his long black cloak flaring in the wind. "I've saved this town four times already. I can do it again."

"Then I'm staying to help you."

He glared at me as if he wanted to throttle me. "Sun and Moon, why are you so stubborn?"

I planted my hands on my hips. "Because you need someone as stubborn as you are to be your wife. No one else would put up with you."

He scowled in reply as the darkness began to move again. From the east more of those shadow beasts emerged and began loping, shambling, or flying toward us. Dozens of them.

Raith and I gathered our spells and began casting at them, over and over, but they kept coming. Soon we were surrounded. A claw tore at my skirt. A fang ripped through Raith's arm. And the darkness only grew stronger.

"There are too many of them," I called out. "We have to make our escape!"

Raith sent a lightning bolt through a flying beast. "We can't leave them here! They'll find another town, one that hasn't already been abandoned."

I bit my lip and nodded as I threw another lash of flame at a crawling shadow beast. When it was nothing but dust, I reached out and took Raith's hand. "Then we'll do it together."

Power flared between us, filling us both with renewed

energy. We summoned fire and lightning together, blasting through all the beasts around us and sending them up in smoke. The magic was so strong it couldn't be contained, and we unleashed it on the rest of the dark-covered town. The fire ate at the shadows like corrosion, burning the darkness away until the buildings underneath were revealed, which instantly burst into flame.

The fire spread quickly across the town and took out the darkness, which let out shrill, inhuman cries. It wasn't long before the entire town was nothing but cinders and smoke. Bellsover was destroyed, but at least the darkness was gone.

"They came from the east," I said, after catching my breath. "Do you think there are more that way in the forest? Should we follow their trail?"

Raith shook his head. "The east is already lost. There's nothing we can do there."

"Are you sure? Perhaps together we could—"

"No!" he snapped. He ran a hand over his face, looking more exhausted than I'd ever seen him. "You've done enough tonight. It's time we returned to the castle."

"All right," I said, though I got the feeling there was something about the east he wasn't telling me. Was that where this darkness had originated from? Perhaps it truly was too dangerous for even Raith to venture into, but if we didn't confront it, how would we ever stop it?

"You need to get some rest anyway." I slid my arm through his. "I'll teleport us back."

He leveled a steely gaze at me. "You? You'll get us trapped in the Shadow Lands."

I rolled my eyes. "I got here, didn't I?"

"Beginner's luck," he muttered.

I snorted and called forth the spell, calling the darkness to me. With Raith at my side it was even easier, as if the shadows were drawn to him. As it covered us whole and blocked out all light, I closed my eyes and pictured my bedroom with its red and black décor and the large windows looking out over the garden.

Home.

When I opened my eyes, we stood a few feet from my bed. I flashed Raith a smile. "See? Not a problem."

Raith stared at me with his brow furrowed. "I can't believe it," he finally said. "You have an affinity for shadow, like I do."

I blinked at him. "I do?"

"That explains how you were able to cast the teleporta-tion spell so easily, a spell that many of the strongest wizards never master in their entire lives. And you taught it to your-self in what, a few hours?"

"Less than that," I said. "But are you certain?"

He rubbed his stubbled jaw as he considered me. "I've never known anyone with the same affinity as me, but yes, I'm sure. That explains why our magic is stronger together too."

It also explained why the darkness had called so strongly to me, and how it had seemed both beautiful and horrifying. "But fire is my other affinity. Doesn't that seem contra-dictory?"

"That's always how it is. My affinities are shadow and

lightning. Yours are shadow and fire. The Archwizard's are stone and air."

Two affinities? It was hard to believe. From what I'd read in Raith's books, very few wizards had more than one—something like one in a thousand, and wizards were rare as it was. Those that had two were among the most powerful of all. I'd never expected to be one of them, but excitement bubbled up inside me along with a sense of satisfied contentment, as if I'd always known this was my destiny.

I was a royal and a wizard, like Raith and my mother, and I was going to make them both proud.

TWENTY-FIVE

RAITH

Rose stood before me in the black gown she'd worn to dinner, the one with the low neckline that had tempted me until I'd been unable to resist touching her breast earlier. Now the gown was torn in three places, a reminder she had barely made it out of Bellsover alive. Her once-perfectly styled hair had dark locks escaping down the nape of her neck and framing her face, which was not scared, regretful, or full of guilt, as it should be. Instead, her amber eyes seemed to dance with a new light.

"Will you teach me shadow magic next?" she asked.

"Not a chance. In fact, I'm strongly regretting teaching you anything at all."

Her brow furrowed. "How can you say such a thing? If it weren't for my help, you'd probably be passed out in the middle of that ruined town right now! Or worse!"

"You shouldn't have been there at all!" I snapped, my

tightly controlled rage finally boiling over. "You're not ready! I've told you that numerous times, but you never listen. Instead, you went behind my back and taught yourself a spell I'd already told you was dangerous, then charged into the middle of a battle against opponents you were not prepared for in the slightest. It's a miracle you made it out alive!"

She propped her hands on her hips, refusing to back down despite my tone. "I *am* ready! I proved that tonight!"

I strode toward her, forcing her to take a step back, until she was pressed against the wall. "You proved you're reckless and foolhardy. Do you even think at all before you rush into things?"

"Why can't you simply accept that you need my help?"

"Because I don't need it!" I pressed my hands to the wall on either side of her head and stared down at her, caging her in. "I've dealt with this threat on my own until now, and that's what I will continue to do."

She looked up at me defiantly. "Not anymore. I'm going with you from now on."

"No, you're not. I will not let you put yourself in harm's way for my sake." My anger grew hotter at the thought of one of those shadowy tendrils dragging her into the darkness. "I forbid you from doing it again."

"You *forbid* it?" She glared at me and all the candles in the room flared brighter. "What makes you think I would listen to you?"

"Nothing. You obviously don't listen to a damn thing I say." I lowered my head until my mouth was almost touching hers. "But I can prevent you in other ways. You still have a lot to learn about magic. I could put a barrier around this entire castle to keep you inside."

"Why?" she asked. "Why won't you let me do this with you?"

"Because I can't stand the thought of losing you too!"

She stared up at me in shock as the words slipped out. I pressed her back against the wall and crushed my mouth against hers, unable to stop myself. I kissed her hard, fueled with anger and lingering fear over what she'd done. But as my tongue slid across hers, the anger turned into pure passion, and she wrapped her arms around my neck and kissed me back with the same intensity. She'd been so reckless tonight, and my chest ached at the thought she would do all of that for me. I didn't deserve such devotion. I didn't want it. But no matter how much I pushed her away and tried to keep my distance, she battered at my walls until she found a way through.

Our kiss deepened, but I still couldn't get enough. I needed to taste more of her. My lips trailed to the spot just below her ear, eliciting a little sigh from her, before I kissed my way down her graceful neck. She arched toward me, her fingers tightening on my shirt, while my mouth lingered just above her collarbone. The view of her cleavage in that black dress beckoned me. This was where I should end things before we went any further. I was about to do just that as my mouth found its way to the spot between the top of her breasts, but her hand slid along the back of my head, holding me there. Demanding even more, like the queen she was. After that, there was no stopping.

I ran my thumbs upon her nipples over the black fabric, feeling how hard they already were, and she let out a soft gasp. The sound was so delicious I couldn't help but want to hear it again and again. I eased her dress down, freeing her left breast, and replaced the fabric with my mouth. Another lovely gasp. I swirled my tongue around her pebbled nipple, and heard my name fall from her lips, as if she were begging. Did she even know what she was begging for?

I claimed her other perfect breast, worshipping it like I'd done the first one, until her breathing was heavy and her fingers gripped my hair tightly. My cock strained at my trousers, but it would have to wait. I had a feeling this was Rose's first time, and I wasn't going to rush it. Not just for her pleasure, but so I could savor every moment with her. It had been three years since I'd been with a woman. Three years since I'd even wanted to be with one. When you'd waited this long, you had to make every second count.

"This dress has been tempting me all night," I said, as I slowly spun her around. "I've been thinking about doing this since dinner."

I yanked on the dress's ties, undoing them with one sharp tug. The gown fell open, revealing the smooth pale skin of her back and shoulders, so delicate and feminine and sensual. She stood tall while I slowly eased the dress down along her slim waist and the wide curves of her hips. It dropped to the floor, leaving her in nothing at all.

I spun her around and took her in, from her full breasts

to the dark mound between her thighs. She gazed at me with a touch of vulnerability as she stood naked before me, but with confidence too. My bold, beautiful queen. My wife.

I'd resisted her for so long, but no more. Tonight she would be mine.

TWENTY-SIX

ROSE

Raith captured my mouth, his hands circling my waist, drawing me close. I pressed myself against him, but the brush of fabric against my bare skin only reminded me that he was still clothed. I grasped his black shirt, pushing it up, and he lifted it over his head and tossed it on the floor. I'd ached to touch his hard chest ever since seeing him sword fighting, and now I slowly smoothed my hands across the ridges and valleys of his muscles. He wasn't as muscular as a guard, but he was long and lean and had a dark trail of hair leading down into his trousers that I very much wanted to explore.

Before I could do just that, Raith swept me up in his arms like he'd done that night he'd tucked me into bed. Except this time I was completely naked and pressed against him, and I could pull his mouth down to mine as he carried me to the bed. He set me on the blankets with care, and then moved over me. I slid my arms around his neck and pulled him down to me, desperate with want. I craved something I'd never had before, something only he could help me with.

"Raith," I gasped, before his mouth found mine again, like our lips were irresistibly drawn together. His tongue swept over mine as his body pressed me down into the bed, surrounding me with his presence. His hard length rubbed against my core, and I moaned. Yes, that was what I needed, more of that. My leg came up and his fingers gripped my thigh, bringing us closer together. If only his trousers weren't in the way.

Raith dipped his head into the curve of my neck and pressed a soft kiss there, then began moving down my body. He stopped at my breasts, his tongue tracing a circle around each hard nipple, until my back arched off the bed and my breathing became ragged. His lips brushed against the soft underside of my breasts as he continued his slow exploration of my body, sending a rush of wet heat between my legs. He kissed his way down my stomach and his every touch was tender and reverent, but when his mouth met the curve of my hip, I gasped his name again.

"Yes, my wife?" he asked, before planting another hot kiss on the spot where my thigh met my hip.

"I need..." I couldn't speak anymore, not when his lips went lower, brushing against my mound.

"I know what you need." He spread my legs wide. "Do you trust me?"

"Always."

His eyes flashed with pure male satisfaction before his

head dropped between my thighs. The first touch of his mouth was so shocking, so exquisite, and so absolutely amazing, I let out a loud cry that I barely recognized as my own. I nearly pulled away at the unexpected sensations coursing through me, but his hands gripped my hips and held me there. His tongue slid along my slippery skin, teasing my folds, tasting me in places no man had ever touched before. Something coiled within me, my need growing stronger, and I buried my hands in his black hair, desperate for more.

The things Raith did with his mouth pushed me closer and closer to the edge. I ached for release, completely at the mercy of my husband, who made me spiral higher with each slide of his tongue. When I thought I might explode at any moment, he slowly dipped one finger inside me, giving me exactly what I'd been missing, as if he truly understood what I needed even more than I did. The pleasure became almost unbearable when he slid in and out of me, before it exploded within me like a spark igniting into a bonfire. My grip tightened in his hair as the climax shuddered through me and never seemed to end.

My body went limp, my mind delirious with pleasure, while Raith stood and began removing his trousers. They slid down his body and I stared at the hard length they revealed, before he made his way up my body again. This time his naked skin slid along my own, and my desire reawakened at the feel of nothing between us.

"That was only the beginning," he said, as he moved between my legs.

"I can't imagine how it could get any better."

A low, sensual laugh rumbled through his chest. "Oh, trust me. It does. It will."

I'd wanted this from the moment we'd met, even if I hadn't realized it yet. Certainly, from the moment we'd been married. Raith had made me wait so long, and he'd pushed me away so many times, I almost worried he would back out again now. I couldn't let that happen.

As the steely length of his arousal settled against my core, I wrapped my legs around him, pulling him closer. "Take me, Raith. I'm yours."

When he entered me with just the tip, his face twisted as if he were in pain even as he let out a groan of pure pleasure. I arched up to take more of him, my body stretching around his thickness, and I tightened my arms around his neck.

He pressed his mouth to my temple. "Relax. I'm not going anywhere this time."

Relief unfurled within me and the anxious tension left my body. He pushed deeper inside, going slowly to let me grow accustomed to his size, until there was no stopping this anymore. Not when he wanted this as much as I did.

When he was buried deep within me and his body was pressed tight against mine, he claimed my mouth in a passionate kiss. He slid his tongue along mine until I was aching with need again, practically whimpering for more. He must have sensed my growing desire because he began to move, and I gasped at the new sensations.

He rocked into me with one long, slow thrust, making

me cry out. But then he paused, deep inside me, his eyes searching mine. Checking if I was in pain, I realized.

"Again," I managed to get out.

With a groan, he slowly pulled almost completely out of me and then slid back inside, making my nerves tingle. He studied my face and I nodded, biting my lip against the tightness within me. It didn't hurt, not exactly, but my body felt stretched to the limit. But at the same time, it craved more.

"Don't stop," I told him.

With those words, he released another groan and began to move again. As my body adjusted to his size, intense passion sparked between us, like when we did magic together. I dug my nails into his back as he began a steady rhythm that brought me back to the brink of pleasure. Our bodies fit together as if we were made for each other, and every touch, every look, and every kiss only confirmed that in my mind.

Then he reached one hand under me, fingers digging into my bottom, and lifted my hips up to him, guiding himself deeper into me. The new angle brought a delicious friction as he pounded into me harder and faster. I lifted my hips to meet him, chasing my pleasure with each thrust.

Suddenly, it was too much, and I convulsed around him as the passion crested and swept through me. My fingers tightened on his bottom, pulling him deeper, as I lost all control of myself and become his completely. He thrust faster, his pace relentless, before he let go with a primal groan that I felt throughout my entire body.

When our bodies stilled, Raith swept me into his arms, cradling me against him. He kissed me with so much tenderness and passion it was hard to believe that earlier tonight we'd been fighting. The brush of his lips against mine made my chest ache with all the things I felt but didn't dare say out loud. If Raith knew the true depths of my feelings for him he would no doubt erect those walls again, and I couldn't let that happen, not when I'd finally brought them crashing down.

"Rose," he muttered into my hair. "Sun and Moon, what you do to me."

"I did nothing." I took his face in my hands so I could gaze into his stormy eyes, which had quieted for the first time since we'd met. I ran my thumbs across the dark stubble on his sharp jaw, loving every inch of him.

He pressed his forehead against mine as he regained control of his breathing. "Are you sore?"

"No, I don't think so." Every inch of me felt tired and stretched and *different*, but I wasn't in any pain. Only deliciously satisfied and relaxed, as if I'd just taken a warm bath.

"Good." He rolled onto his side and pulled me into his arms, molding me against his body. "You might be sore tomorrow though."

"Then you'll just have to ease my aches, won't you?"

"I'll do my best." He pressed a kiss to my bare shoulder that was so tender it made my heart ache. His earlier words came back to me: *I can't stand the thought of losing you too.* These feelings of love and intimacy were new to me, but he'd felt them before with his previous wife, before she'd been stolen from him. I assumed it was one of the reasons he'd been so hesitant to take me to bed. Had he put those worries aside, or did they still trouble him?

"Have you been with anyone since your wife?" I asked, while his hands idly stroked my back.

"No. There was no one before her, and no one after her. Only you."

His words made me warm inside and I pressed a kiss to his lips. I didn't mind sharing his heart with Silena. I understood that he would always love her, and I accepted that. I only hoped he could love me too. Someday.

TWENTY-SEVEN

RAITH

I woke with a woman in my arms for the first time
in years.

I lay on my side with Rose in front of me, my body
curled behind hers. Her bottom was flush against my hips,
while my hand rested on her thigh. The feel of her naked
skin against mine was already stirring my cock to attention. I
couldn't help but slide my fingers along her soft curves while
I pressed a kiss to her shoulder. Even though the sun was
peeking inside the bedroom curtains and a thousand tasks
awaited me, I had no desire to move. Hang the kingdom, I
could spend a few more minutes with my wife without it all
falling apart.

She stirred and turned her head toward me, giving me a
sleepy, seductive smile. I captured her mouth with mine
before she could say a word, while my fingers tightened

around her thigh, pulling her against me. She pushed back toward me, no doubt feeling how hard I was for her, surprising me with how quickly she succumbed to desire.

I let my lips trail across her neck while moving a hand to her breasts. I couldn't help myself, not when her naked and willing body was pressed against mine. All I could think about was being inside her again. That taste of her last night hadn't been enough. No, it had just been the start.

As I sucked and nibbled on her neck, she became pliant under my touch, tilting her head back as she moaned. My fingers slid down her stomach, along her hips, and then made their way between her thighs. She hitched her leg up, parting wider for me, and knowing she wanted this only made me need her even more. She was already so wet for me and let out a soft moan as I slid one finger inside. I knew we should wait, that she might be tender after last night, but I couldn't stop myself, not when she was begging for me to claim her.

I aligned my cock with her entrance and slid inside in one smooth thrust. She gasped, and for a second I worried I'd hurt her, but then her hips pushed back against me, taking me deeper. Wild lust filled me at the feel of being within her again and at her obvious desire, and I grabbed her leg and hooked it behind my own, spreading her wide. The perfect position for me to use my fingers to please her while filling her from behind.

We didn't say a single word as lust took control of our bodies. She reached back and tangled her fingers in my hair as breathy moans escaped her lips with each thrust. I rubbed her clit at the same time, heightening her bliss, while I claimed her body as my own. All she could do was push her hips back against me and accept the pleasure I gave her.

I took her harder and faster until she was calling out my name and tightening around me, her body shuddering with release. Her soft cries pushed me over the edge only seconds later, and I clung to her tightly as I let go with one final thrust. I buried my face in her hair and caressed her breasts, as lingering traces of pleasure shuddered through us both.

Only when my lust was sated did I realize I'd been crushing her body against mine, and that I'd been more rough and forceful than I'd intended. I withdrew from Rose's body and cradled her in my arms. "I apologize. You must be sore. I simply couldn't help myself."

Silena had been sore after our wedding night. Of course, I'd been a lot younger and less experienced then. I hadn't yet known how to please a woman properly or how to prepare her for my entry. Silena and I had learned together after that night.

Silena. The thought of her was like a dagger in my heart. I'd pledged myself to her forever, and now I'd slept with another woman. Even though Silena was gone, it felt like a betrayal. I shouldn't even be thinking about her while I was in bed with Rose. Guilt wracked my body with a shudder and conflict warred within me. Not only guilt for sleeping with Rose, but guilt for thinking of Silena at a moment like this too. My heart was torn between the two women who owned it. The one I'd lost, and the one I was terrified to lose now.

"I'm not sore. I feel amazing." She pressed a kiss to my jaw, oblivious to my tormented thoughts. "We should stay in bed all day. No one would miss us."

"We both know that isn't true." I let my fingers tighten around her thigh for the briefest moment, but then I eased away from her. "As tempting as your offer is, I must be going."

With a sigh, she asked, "Already? It's barely dawn."

As I stood, my gaze wandered slowly across her beautiful naked curves, and I was tempted to climb back in bed with her. But no, the conflict within me was too great, and the urge to escape too strong. Even Rose's lovely smile and tempting body couldn't overcome the burden settling over my shoulders.

"I'll see you at supper," I said, before turning away.

I went through the connecting door to my bedroom, where I quickly washed up and donned some clothes, my thoughts tormenting me the entire time. I couldn't go on like this, torn between my two wives. And avoiding Rose wouldn't work—I'd tried that already and failed. Even if I could withstand the temptation to be with her, I needed an heir soon.

My fists clenched at the thought of my cousin. He wanted to take my kingdom, and Rose with it. Let him try. I'd burn off every inch of his skin while he was still alive so he could smell himself going up into flames. Silena's blood was on his hands, and even though Rose wanted to use him to get knowledge of future plots, all I could think of was revenge. No, not revenge. *Justice.*

I stormed through the castle, my mood so dour all the servants shied away from me at the sight of my face. Even Oren kept his distance.

There was only one place for me to go to ease my troubles.

I teleported outside to a secluded part of the garden I rarely visited. The sun had barely breached the horizon, casting faint light across the stones in front of me. I slowly walked among them, the tall grass brushing against my cloak as I gazed down at the graves.

My mother.

My father.

My wife.

All of them buried here, along with previous members of the royal line. My entire family. All of it...until now.

I kneeled in front of Silena's grave and stared at the headstone. Red roses had grown up around it, despite my insistence on removing them from the castle's grounds. The irony was not lost on me.

I let my hand brush over the grass covering her grave. "Forgive me," I said, closing my eyes as emotion became a torrent inside me. Grief, guilt, regret, anger, and love burned me from the inside out.

"There's nothing to forgive, Raith," Silena's voice said, in my mind. I could easily picture her as if she were still alive, as if not a day had gone by. She'd flash me her serene smile, her golden hair sparkling under the morning light.

"There is. I've taken another woman to bed."

"She is your wife," she'd say. Silena had always been practical, and little had riffled her feathers. She would have made an excellent queen.

I nodded, bowing my head. "I care for her too. I'm sorry."

"You still love me, do you not?"

"Of course. I always will."

"There is room in your heart for both of us." At this point she would take my hands and smile up at me. "Raith, you've lost so much in your life, and I understand why you've closed yourself off to love and surrounded yourself in darkness. But perhaps it's time to allow yourself a bit of happiness and light for a change."

I could hear her voice as clear as if she was standing in front of me, and when the roses fluttered under the breeze, I felt her words in my heart. Even though it was all in my head, I knew Silena would tell me to move on. She would want me to be happy. She would want what was best for Ilidan. And she would have liked Rose a lot. But could I truly move on? Could I accept love again and live with the threat of losing it a second time?

The darkness was all around us, growing stronger every night. How could I offer my heart to Rose knowing the danger we faced and what I might have to sacrifice to stop it?

Only when my kingdom was safe could I entertain the thought of loving Rose the way she deserved. I couldn't afford to be distracted by her right now, not with so much at stake, and I couldn't let her rush into danger again. She was headstrong and reckless, and even if I trapped her inside the castle, she'd find a way around my magic eventually. There was only one option—I had to find the Shadow Lord and stop him before he could hurt her too.

Tonight this had to end, one way or another.

TWENTY-EIGHT

ROSE

I stared at a drawing of a tall, shadowy figure in all black, before shaking my head and turning the page. I'd spent my day combing through dozens of books in the library searching for information on the Shadow Lord, but there was depressingly little to be found other than speculation, rumor, and myth. With a sigh, I slammed the old tome shut and grabbed the next one in the pile.

It probably didn't help that I kept finding myself staring off into space, remembering the things Raith had done to me last night and this morning. Carnal, passionate, wonderful things. Things I wanted to experience again and again. Hopefully starting tonight after supper.

A few hours later I closed up the books and rushed to our private dining room early, unable to contain my impatience or my excitement to see Raith again. The room was empty except for the servants and guards, but that was to be expected. I adjusted my cleavage and smoothed my dress as I waited, hoping he would find me as appealing as he had last night.

But when he entered the room, he barely spared me a glance. I offered him a warm smile, but he ignored it completely. He sat across from me and grabbed his napkin without a word, a harsh scowl on his lips. A crack ran through my heart as I realized nothing had changed between us. Where was the man from last night and this morning, who had treated me like a treasure he'd been searching for all his life?

"Raith," I said, hating this silence between us.

His hard eyes finally slid to mine. "Rose."

Words hung on the tip of my tongue, but nothing came out. I'd thought things would be different after last night, that we would finally be husband and wife in every sense of the word. But Raith was as distant and cold as always, wrapped up in his own thoughts, unwilling to let me behind those walls he'd erected. I wanted to ask him if sleeping together meant as much to him as it did to me, but I wasn't sure I could take his rejection, not tonight.

I bowed my head and began sipping at my soup, trying not to show the crack spreading across my heart. "I haven't seen you all day."

"I've been busy."

Not in his study or his workshop though. I'd stopped by both of those a few times during the day. Yes, I realized how pathetic that sounded. I'd become a lovesick fool, and I didn't know how to stop myself. And Raith didn't seem to return those feelings, which meant I would be doomed to suffer this unrequited love for the rest of our days.

"So I noticed," I said, trying to hide the despair from my voice. "I spent the day in the library looking for information on the Shadow Lord, but was unsuccessful."

"I told you not to bother," he replied, his words clipped. "I can assure you I've scoured through them all."

I lifted one bare shoulder in a shrug. "I had to try."

"I appreciate your determination, but I already told you I don't want you involved in this."

My hands clenched on my skirts as I gave him a defiant stare. "I'm already involved whether you like it or not. We both know you have a better chance of stopping this darkness with my help. You can't deny my affinities are useful, almost as if fate brought the two of us together to fight this battle."

I wondered if my mother had seen this very thing in her fortune runes, and if everything she'd set up with Dahlia had led me to this point. The rightness of it burned within my chest. I'd always wanted more from life—to learn magic, to fall in love, to travel, and to do something good for the world. This was my moment, here, now, with Raith. Why didn't he see that?

His eyes narrowed. "I fight my battles alone."

"Not anymore."

He threw down his napkin and rose to his feet. "I'm done arguing about this, Rose."

I jumped up and crossed the room to him, my despair

shifting to fury. "Then concede that I am right and you are wrong."

"Never." He caught my face in his hands and pressed a rough, open-mouthed kiss to my lips. I gasped in surprise, but then my fingers tore at his shirt, drawing him closer as I kissed him back with the same passion. His tongue swept across mine, his teeth tugged at my lower lip, and heat flashed between my legs. I wanted to shove our plates aside and beg him to take me right there on the table.

"Stubborn wife," he said, between kisses.

"Insufferable husband," I replied.

As he pulled back, he caressed my face and gazed into my eyes. "I must go."

His words hit me like a blow to the stomach. "Go? Now? Where?"

He dropped his hands, his face growing somber. "I won't let this nightmare go on any longer. Tonight I go to face the Shadow Lord."

"What?" I cried. "You can't. Raith, no. Don't do this!"

"I've determined it's the only way. Nothing else I've done has worked."

"Then let me go with you!"

"No."

I grabbed onto his arm, desperate to keep him from teleporting away. "Raith, I'm begging you. You must let me come!"

"I said no." He pressed his forehead against mine, and his fingers stroked my cheek. "Please, Rose. You're all I have left."

I fell silent, my eyes wide at his confession. For once, he'd shocked the words right out of my mouth. Finally, I managed, "You do care about me."

"Foolish girl." He drew me into his arms, clutching me against his chest while he buried his face in my hair. "I care about you too much."

I turned to brush my lips against his cheek. "I care about you too, Raith. That's why I had to find you last night even though it was dangerous. If you hadn't come back, I would have been lost too. Which is why I'm going with you now, whether you like it or not."

"No, you're not." He released me and straightened up to loom over me, but he didn't intimidate me.

I planted my hands on my hips. "You can't stop me."

A cruel smile touched his lips. "Oh, but I can. I've put up wards to prevent you from teleporting outside the castle grounds."

My mouth fell open as the fury returned, but I quickly recovered and stared him down with fire in my eyes. "I'll find a way to break through them."

"I know you will, but not tonight." He pressed a quick kiss to my angry lips, before the darkness surrounded him.

"Raith!" I screamed, my heart breaking apart as the shadows grew. "Stop!"

But he was already gone.

I tried to teleport after him, drawing the complicated rune and focusing on his presence, but was hit by an invisible wall. I gritted my teeth and tried again, but nothing I did could break through Raith's wards. I kicked his chair in sheer frustration, but all that did was make my toe hurt. That impossible man! How dare he trap me in this castle while he left to risk his life in foolish ways. If he thought I was going to stay put and wait quietly while he went to face the Shadow Lord, then he didn't know me well at all.

Though I was no longer hungry, I grabbed a chunk of bread off my neglected plate and shoved it in my mouth before leaving the room. I had to keep my strength up if I was going to find a way to save my infuriating husband.

I stomped over to his workshop, hoping to find something that would tell me how to defeat his wards, but the door refused to open, even with magic. What now?

I couldn't give up. I wouldn't. Not when he was out there risking his life to save this kingdom. Not when I finally knew he cared for me.

Raith's words came back to me again and I was struck with an idea. I couldn't teleport from inside the castle grounds...but what if I left them? He couldn't ward the entire kingdom.

I spun around with my new plan in mind and came face to face with Oren. Perfect. "Oren, I need a horse readied for me at once and—"

"I'm sorry, your majesty, but the King has ordered us not to let you leave the castle."

"Of course he did." Damn that husband of mine. Still, I wouldn't be thwarted. He probably believed he'd thought of everything, but he'd never grown up with five sisters and an overbearing father who never wanted us to have any fun. I sighed in an overly dramatic fashion. "I'm just so worried about him."

"As am I." His brow furrowed. "But my duty is to make sure you are safe."

"I understand," I said, in a defeated voice. "I suppose there is nothing for me to do except retire to my rooms and pray to the Sun and Moon for his quick return."

Oren gave me a curt nod. "That might be best for all of us."

I brushed past him and walked down the long, brightly-lit hall, already coming up with a new plan. As soon as I stepped into my room, I sent Loura away, claiming I had a headache and only wished to be alone despite her protests that she should help me undress or pour me a bath. Once she was gone I grabbed my cloak, threw the hood over my head, and opened my bedroom window. I glanced outside, searching the gardens for any sign of the Shadow Lord. When I didn't see a dark figure skulking about, I hefted up my skirts and climbed out onto the ledge.

When I was younger, I'd done things like this all the time to escape my own castle and my father's strict rules, both by myself and with my other sisters. Lily had always hovered inside, telling me it was too dangerous and that I was surely going to get caught. I never did though. And I wouldn't tonight either.

With a quick rune I'd learned earlier today, I gathered shadows around myself, blocking out the ever-present light from the nearby torches so none of the guards on patrol would see me. Once I was confident I was hidden I stepped onto the large tree outside my window, grasping onto its thick, rough bark. With less grace than I cared to admit I slowly made my way down, careful not to snag my gown on anything or make a sound.

I nearly turned my ankle when I hit the ground, but then I straightened my back, adjusted my hood, and set off into the garden. Nothing was going to stop me tonight. Not the wards. Not Raith. And not the Shadow Lord either.

I made my way across the castle grounds and through the gardens, which were beautiful under the starlight. It was a pity none could enjoy them, not when everyone was so fearful of the dark. I swore to the Moon that once all of this was over, Raith and I would throw nighttime parties outside to celebrate the Celestials. After all, why should only the Sun get its due in Ilidan?

I neared the edge of the garden, where my only obstacle was a tall stone wall I would have to climb over, but I sensed something behind me. A dark, terrible presence that sucked up all the light around us. With my heart in my throat, I slowly turned and gazed up at the towering figure before me, composed of swirling shadows and inky darkness.

The Shadow Lord.

TWENTY-NINE

ROSE

All I could do was stare at the tall beast in front of me, shaped like a man but made of magic even blacker than night. Wispy tendrils of shadow danced off his shoulders and drifted from his fingertips. Great, pointed wings rose from his back, and his eyes crackled with white lightning. The Shadow Lord was terrifyingly beautiful and inhuman, radiating so much power it made my hands tremble, but I couldn't back down.

"Where is Raith?" I called out. "What have you done with him?"

"Raith." The monster's voice was cold and jarring, like the scrape of claws against glass. "Raith is gone."

"Gone?" I stumbled back and pressed a hand to my stomach, overwhelmed by worry. No, it wasn't possible. Gone didn't necessarily mean *gone*. But what if Raith had already fought him and failed? Was the Shadow Lord here to collect on the kingdom and everything else my husband had once held dear?

No. Not while I lived. He would have to get through me first.

I moved to stand in front of him, digging my heels into the soft ground while I raised my hands to cast what runes I could. I had no idea if my husband was dead or alive. For all I knew, he could be out there looking for the Shadow Lord now. And if not... Well, if Raith couldn't defeat the Shadow Lord with all of his magic and knowledge then I had little hope of it myself, but I wouldn't run away. There was no one else to fight for Ilidan except me. I was Queen now, and I would die before I let the darkness claim my kingdom.

"Move aside," the Shadow Lord commanded.

"Never." I cast the rune for fire and summoned bright flames in each of my palms. "Go back to the Shadow Lands and leave this kingdom alone!"

I sent the fire toward his chest, but he swatted it away with a thick, black hand tipped with sharp claws. The flames seared through some of his fingers, making the shadows break apart like wispy clouds, but then they reformed instantly. My throat clenched, but I summoned more fire, casting the runes in my mind as I rapidly unleashed magic at his chest. The dark beast let out a roar that made my skin crawl as the flames burned through his shadowy skin, but every time I hit him the damage quickly healed.

His large claws swooped down and knocked me aside before I could conjure more magic. I fell flat on my back in the damp grass, the impact forcing the air from my lungs, but I wasn't injured. I sucked in a ragged gasp as I pushed myself up, preparing for another blow, but it never came. Why wasn't he attacking me with his magic? Or tearing me apart with those claws? Was he dragging this moment out to torture me further?

"Return to the castle," his icy voice demanded.

I was getting really tired of people telling me what to do. I scrambled to my feet, ripping the skirt of my dress as my boot snagged on it, and raised my chin defiantly. "I will not."

Remembering Raith's teachings, I traced the rune in my head and added my own flourish to the design, imbuing it with my willpower before letting it go. A ring of flame circled around the Shadow Lord's neck, squeezing tight. He raised his hand to put the fire out, but it tore through the darkness nearly faster than he could heal it. Nearly.

With a horrible screech he backhanded me again, sending me tumbling to the ground once more. As the fire was snuffed out he towered over me, and I felt pure, primal fear like I'd never known before. Dark, inky claws wrapped around me, pinning my arms to my sides, and though I tried to fight back I knew this would be the end. My magic did little to harm the Shadow Lord, and I'd failed to protect my kingdom. My one consolation was that Raith was probably waiting for me in the Celestial Lands already.

I squeezed my eyes shut as the shadows tightened around me, and I whispered the words that would be my last. "Forgive me, Raith. I love you."

The Shadow Lord paused. My death never came. The darkness retreated.

I opened my eyes as the inky black tendrils pulled away and the Shadow Lord's body began to grow smaller, as if contracting in on itself. I shuffled backward on my hands and knees, desperately trying to catch my breath while wondering what new horror I would face next. But as the Shadow Lord shrank away and his darkness dissipated, he left only a man in his place. He collapsed to the ground, seemingly unconscious.

A new kind of horror gripped me as I crawled toward the fallen man. A man with raven-black hair, eyes the color of an angry storm, and lips I hadn't been able to stop thinking about. A sob escaped my throat as I wrapped my arms around him, pulling him to my chest. He was breathing, but it was shallow, and his skin was ice-cold. Worst of all was the revelation that we'd been wrong all along, and the threat was far worse than I could have imagined.

It wasn't the Shadow Lord who was attacking Ilidan.

It was Raith.

THIRTY

RAITH

Rose's voice beckoned me out of the darkness. She called my name over and over with a ragged cry, and the sound wrapped around my soul and yanked me back to reality. Her arms held me tight, her face pressed into my hair, and her body trembled slightly. I lifted my hands to embrace her back, but weariness slowed my movements and dragged me down. I opened my eyes and breathed in her sweet scent, along with the cool freshness of the moonlit garden around us.

"Rose," I said, my voice ragged. "What are we doing out here?"

She touched my face and stared at me with relief, along with something else. Something like fear. "Raith! Oh, thank the Sun and Moon."

I coughed, trying to clear the dryness in my throat as I sat up. My entire body ached, and I felt as though all my energy had been stolen from me. I pressed a hand to my forehead and tried to remember how I'd ended up here. I'd decided the only thing to do was to confront the Shadow Lord, but since he wouldn't face me in my kingdom, I'd planned to find him in his own realm. Teleporting away from Rose was the last thing I remembered. Had I found the Shadow Lord? How had I wound up in the garden?

I reached out and touched a lingering tear on Rose's cheek, wiping it away. "What is it, Rose?"

She shook her head, biting her lip. "We can't speak of it here. Remove the wards around the castle so I can teleport us inside."

I nearly protested or tried to teleport us myself, but I was too weak and she knew it. I'd barely made it back to the castle the other night when I'd woken up in a strange place with no memories, but I was even worse off now. I raised my hand and slowly traced the rune to break the spell preventing her from teleporting on castle grounds, and then nodded.

She wrapped her arms around me and the darkness embraced us like an old friend. When it receded, we were on my bed. She helped me get comfortable against the pillows, and then sat beside me, gazing down at me with an unreadable expression. She was normally so open with her thoughts and feelings, and it unnerved me that I couldn't tell what was going on in that lovely mind of hers.

"Explain," I demanded. "How did we get in the garden? Why are you so upset?"

She let out a long, shuddering sigh, but then began to

speak. "I saw the Shadow Lord outside the castle again. This time, I confronted him."

"You did what?" I started to get up, but she pressed a hand to my chest and pushed me back down. "What were you thinking?"

"I was thinking I needed to find you. And I did."

"I was there?" I ran a hand through my hair, wracking my brain for the lost memory. "I must have confronted the Shadow Lord and somehow ended up there. How did you escape him?"

Her eyes were serious as they stared back at me. "I didn't."

"What do you mean?"

"The Shadow Lord let me go. And then he transformed back into a man." She swallowed. "Raith, the Shadow Lord is you."

I stared at her. "I don't understand."

She went on, as though I hadn't said a word. "Or rather, the thing we thought was the Shadow Lord is actually you. For all I know, the actual Shadow Lord is still ruling his own realm. Or maybe he doesn't exist at all. No one seems to know for certain."

I held up a hand, overwhelmed by her rapid words. "That doesn't make any sense. How can I be the Shadow Lord?"

"I don't know. I was hoping you would remember something."

"I don't, and there's no way I can be him. If I am, it

means I'm the one who has been terrorizing the kingdom for the last few years. I would never do that."

"Not intentionally, no," she said, her voice laced with sadness.

"This is absurd," I said. "You must be mistaken."

But slowly my mind began to clear and some of the things in my past started to make sense. The darkness only began to appear after my first wife's murder. Many people had spotted the Shadow Lord spreading the darkness across the land, but I was never able to hunt him down or confront him myself, no matter how hard I looked for him. All I saw was the aftermath of his attacks. My own magic was able to send the darkness back to the Shadow Lands, but I grew weaker every day while the enemy grew stronger. It was a losing battle...a battle I seemed to be fighting against myself. Sun and Moon, could she be right? Was I the monster destroying my own kingdom?

"I need to get to my workshop," I said, as I stumbled to my feet.

Rose reached for my arm. "You need to rest."

"Not until we know if your claims are true or not." I jerked away from her and left the room with the last of my strength.

Rose quickly caught up to me, a frown on her soft lips. "What do you plan to do?"

I shook my head, and the only sound was from my boots as they left harsh footsteps on the stone. I was too busy thinking of all the times I'd woken in my study, unable to recall if I'd slept or not, with no memory of where my evening had gone. I'd chalked it up to exhaustion, but could it be more than that?

I removed the spell locking the workship and we both stepped inside. I searched my shelves until I found a thick purple tonic. While Rose watched, I popped off the stopper and downed the entire bottle in one gulp, cringing at the bitter taste with a hint of lavender.

"What is that?" Rose asked, her eyes both curious and afraid.

"A tonic to help with memory." I grabbed a stool and sank down onto it as the magic began to spread through me, making my head spin. "I need a few moments of silence."

She nodded and sat beside me, her hand lightly resting on my back as I closed my eyes and focused on breathing. Her gentle touch anchored me as snippets of memories began to whisk through my mind. Darkness surrounding me and overwhelming me until I couldn't breathe anymore, while harsh laughter filled my ears. Towering over the town of Haversham with inky shadows leaping from my fingers to cover the buildings there. Watching as people screamed and fled from me in terror. Wrapping my large, shadowy hand around Rose and seeing the fear in her eyes, before she whispered that she loved me.

Sun and Moon, it was all true. I was the one terrorizing Ilidan, not the Shadow Lord. I was destroying its towns and threatening my own people. I'd nearly killed the woman I would do anything to protect. And there was no way to protect her, not when *I* was the danger.

When the memories receded, I found myself with my head in my hands, tearing at my hair. Exhaustion settled over me again, and my mind was flayed and bloody, torn apart by this new revelation. I was no longer a king or a wizard, but a hollow shell of a man who no longer knew who he was.

I met Rose's eyes. "You're right. It is me. Sun and Moon help us all."

"Oh, Raith. I'm sorry." She reached for me, but I pulled back. She frowned and placed her hands in her lap instead. "Do you remember how or why this started? Or what is causing it?"

"No, I was only able to recover a few memories, only brief fragments and glimpses of my time as that...beast."

We sat in defeated silence for a minute, but then Rose drew in a breath and straightened up, gathering her determination again. "I know this is a shock and that it's hard to accept, but it's a good thing we found the truth. Now we can do something about it."

I let out a harsh laugh. "Do something? What can we do?"

"We'll figure out why this is happening and stop it together, of course."

Even after seeing my true nature and the darkness inside of me, she wanted to help. She was so strong, and far too good for a man like me. I couldn't lose her too, not like I'd lost Silena. Especially when *I* was the threat to her life. "No, we won't."

"Raith..."

I gave her my coldest stare. "I don't need or want your help. This is my problem, and I will deal with it alone."

As expected, that only made Rose square her shoulders to face me back defiantly. "It is not yours alone. This is my kingdom too, and has been ever since you married me."

"Marrying you was a mistake. One that must be corrected now."

Her face paled. "What are you saying?"

"I'm saying it's time for you to go back home to Talador. I don't want you here." Lies, lies, lies, but getting her away from me was the only thing that would keep her safe. Even if each word felt bitter on my tongue, and I was tempted to take them all back.

"I don't believe that." She reached for me again and I stepped back.

"Don't touch me!" I snapped.

"All right, I'm sorry. But what about last night?"

I waved a dismissive hand. "It didn't mean anything. Not to me anyway."

She scowled at me. "Raith, I know you're trying to push me away again, but I won't let you do that. You need me, just as much as I need you."

I turned away from her. "I don't need you, and I don't want you in my castle any longer. Like I told you before, I will never love you. You're a fool to think this could be anything real. Now get out." Her mouth fell open, but she didn't move. I glared at her. "Go!"

She pressed a hand to her chest, like I'd physically wounded her there, and then she fled the room in a whoosh of dark skirts. My heart shuddered as the door slammed behind her, even as I tried to convince myself this was for the best. I was a danger to everyone around me, and Rose had to stay away.

It was the only way to keep her safe.

THIRTY-ONE

ROSE

I choked back my tears as I stumbled through the castle, my eyes blurring as I tried to find my way back to my room. I knew Raith didn't mean what he'd said, but his words still hurt...and perhaps there was some truth to them. We'd shared something intimate last night, but that didn't mean he loved me or that he ever would. Maybe he was too broken after Silena's death, and no matter how hard I tried to tear down his walls he would only erect new ones. But I would keep trying, no matter how much it hurt. I didn't know what else to do. I loved him, even if he didn't love me in return. And no matter what he said, I knew in my heart he couldn't defeat the darkness inside him without my help.

I came to an abrupt halt when I rounded a corner and nearly collided with Oren, whose face was flushed as though he'd been rushing around. I quickly brushed a hand across

my cheek to wipe away any remaining tears. "Oren, is everything all right?"

"I've been looking for you." He held out a small enve-
lope with a snowflake seal in the royal blue of Talador. "An
urgent message arrived from your sister, Princess Lily."

I frowned as I opened the seal, removed the letter, and
began to read—but as I did, the tears returned to my eyes.
My father was sick, Lily wrote. He'd fallen into a sudden
coma and no one could get him to awaken, nor could figure
out what ailed him. Every day his breathing grew weaker
and his skin paler. She urged me to come home immediately,
before it was too late.

"I must go," I told Oren, who only nodded as I raced
away. The letter had been sent days ago, and I had to hurry.

I fled to my bedroom, grabbed my thicker cloak from my
closet and whisked it about my shoulders, then switched my
muddy slippers for some heavier boots. With the wards still
down, I closed my eyes and focused on the castle where I'd
grown up as I gathered the darkness around me. Within
seconds, I felt the air grow bitterly cold and the scent of frost
filled my nose, and when I opened my eyes, I was outside in
the forest where I'd first met Raith. Teleporting anywhere
closer would have been too difficult with the castle's wards,
as Raith had told me back then.

I shivered as I made my way toward the castle, my boots
crunching through the snow. How quickly I'd grown used to
the relative warmth of Ilidan and forgotten how cold my
childhood home could be. I started to draw the rune for fire,

but then remembered where I was. Magic was still banned in Talador, even if the King was ill.

The guards took notice of me as I approached, and by the time I stepped inside the white walls of the castle, Aunt Dahlia was already waiting for me. She wore a gray mourning veil, and I choked back a sob at the sight of it. I was already too late.

Her eyes were rimmed with pain and exhaustion as she threw her arms around me. "You came."

I pressed my face into her shoulder, hugging her tight. "I left as soon as I received the message, but I wasn't fast enough."

"I'm sorry, Rose. He passed this morning. There was nothing we could do." She patted my back, her voice heavy with sadness. "Come, I'll take you to him."

As we moved through the castle, I saw other tell-tale signs of grief. Somber gray clothes, eyes cast downward, and a quiet hush that had befallen everyone, as if speaking too loudly might disturb the dead. I struggled to hold myself together as we kept walking.

"Where are your things?" Dahlia asked. "And what happened to your gown?"

I glanced down at myself and saw what she meant. My dress was ripped and covered in dirt and grass stains from fighting Raith earlier. "I didn't bring anything. I was in such a rush I teleported here immediately."

Her eyebrows darted up. "You teleported?"

"Yes, Raith has been teaching me magic."

"I want to hear all about your past few weeks in Ilidan. Later, of course."

My throat clenched. I couldn't think about Ilidan and Raith right now. "Of course."

We stopped outside the heavy double doors that led to my father's private chambers, which I'd been inside only a handful of times. A guard opened them for us, and we entered a room darkened by thick curtains, with only a few flickering candles around my father's bed to light the way. His skin was as white as the walls of the palace, and his eyes were closed and sunken. Lily sat beside him with her head bowed, the gray veil covering much of her features. Keane stood against the wall a few feet away, watching over her as always.

She jumped up when she saw me and rushed into my arms with a soft cry. "Oh, Rose. Thank the Sun and Moon you're here."

"I'm here. I only wish I'd made it in time to say good-bye." I clutched her tightly as emotion made my eyes fill with tears again.

"I'll leave the two of you alone to grieve," Dahlia said, before exiting the room.

I squeezed Lily again and then finally released her. "How did this happen?"

"No one knows. It came on suddenly after dinner one night. The medics thought it could be poison...or magic. But nothing they tried helped him, and every day he grew weaker and weaker until he was gone." She swallowed, her face stoic, though I saw the grief in her eyes. "At least he went quietly in his sleep without any pain."

I nodded, wiping at my face. "How are you doing? And the other girls?"

"As well as can be expected," she said. "Our sisters each mourn in their own way. I've been trying to hold myself together for their sakes, but I must confess I've been falling apart the second I'm alone."

"Of course you are. You always look after us." I hugged her again, trying to send some strength into her thin frame. "But you don't have to be strong for me, Lily. Just let it out."

"Thank you, Rose." She leaned against me for a moment, then sighed and wiped at her eyes as she pulled back. "The entire kingdom is going to be watching me, and I need to be strong. I'm going to be queen soon, after all."

It didn't seem fair that she was forced to lead a kingdom while also grieving, but that was her duty. We were orphans now, and she would soon be coronated. She would undoubtably be a better ruler than our father, but it still seemed too soon for this to happen.

I squeezed her hand. "Don't worry about any of that just yet. Take it day by day. For now, you only need to grieve."

She nodded and we sat beside our father's body as she rested her head on my shoulder, her hands entwined with mine. Tears rolled down my face as I thought of all the things I wished I'd said to Father before Raith had whisked me away to Ilidan. I had so many regrets about the way we'd left things, and I wondered if he'd felt the same. I wasn't sure if we'd have ever been able to mend our relationship, but now I'd never have the chance to try. It was a harsh reminder that life was short and fleeting, and I had a strong desire to run back to Raith to confess my feelings for him.

I stifled the urge immediately. Telling Raith how I felt would only make things worse. No, it was better if he never knew the truth. And though I worried about Ilidan, Raith refused to accept my help in stopping the darkness, and I'd grown weary of fighting with him about it. I wasn't giving up on him or on Ilidan, but I was needed here, and here I would stay. For now, at least.

THIRTY-TWO

RAITH

I jerked awake when sunlight began streaming through my window, my heart already pounding. I was on top of my bed, still wearing my clothes and shoes, my head throbbing. Memories of last night came back, searing me with pain. Sun and Moon, what had I done?

I hauled myself out of bed and went to the door connecting my room with Rose's, but when I threw it open, she wasn't there. The bed was still made, signaling that she hadn't slept in it all night. I crossed into the other room of her suite, checking to make sure she was truly gone, and then I stood in the center of her space feeling lost and more alone than ever before.

I'd told Rose to leave. I'd pushed her away. I'd said I didn't love her or need her. Of course she was gone now. She'd probably teleported back to Talador to be with her family in her own kingdom. My heart clenched painfully, and I tried to remind myself this was what I'd wanted. I was a monster, and she was safer away from me. Even if the loss of her made me feel like a hollow shell.

I dragged in a ragged breath as I left her room. Now that I knew the truth about the darkness, I had to act quickly. For years I'd been looking for the beast terrorizing my kingdom, trying to find a way to stop him, but *I* was the beast. And I had to be stopped.

I didn't know what had caused me to become this monster, but I had a suspicion it had something to do with Silena's death. The darkness had started attacking the kingdom not long after that so it seemed only logical, but knowing the two events were somehow connected didn't give me any clues about how to stop it from continuing. My shadow magic was part of the problem, but that was all I knew.

Once in my workshop, I tore through books, looking for a solution to this new problem or for reports of something like this happening before. After countless hours spent hunched over dusty old tomes, I finally admitted defeat. There was nothing in any of them that recounted a similar situation, and no hints as to how to end it.

I left my workshop and entered my study, where the light was already fading. Night would soon fall, and when that happened, everyone around me would be in danger. It was becoming clear there was only one way to protect my kingdom.

I had to be contained. Every night. For the rest of my life.

Oren appeared in the doorway. "There you are. I wanted to inform you that the Queen has returned to Talador—"

"Yes, I know," I snapped. "It's for the best."

He nodded. "Did the two of you fight? She seemed upset."

I waved a hand. "It doesn't matter. I need you to bring me some moonroot immediately. As much as you can find." I strode from the room with a quick step, knowing Oren would match my pace. "After that, find us a way to keep a constant supply in the castle. We're going to need a lot of it."

Oren's brow furrowed. "Moonroot? Correct me if I'm wrong, but doesn't that prevent wizards from using their magic?"

"It does, yes."

His lips pressed into a tight, disapproving line. "Are you planning to use it on Queen Rose?"

"What? No, of course not." I led us down stone steps that would take us below the castle, into cold, dark depths I rarely visited. "I plan to use it on myself."

"Yourself?"

I ignored his startled question as we entered the dungeons. A foul, decrepit smell made its way to my nose, and torches were the only light down here. We'd need more of those tonight.

I turned to the guard who seemed to be in charge, who

blinked at me in surprise. "I need to see your most secure prison cell. Preferably one that can hold a wizard."

The guard bowed, while Oren's entire body tensed at my question. "Of course, your majesty. Right this way."

The guard led us past numerous prison cells, most of them empty. We stopped at the end of the dungeon in front of a heavy stone door covered in chains. The guard picked out one of his keys and began unlocking the door. "This was built to hold wizards and magical creatures, or so I'm told. It hasn't been used in some time."

He tugged the door open and it scraped against the floor with a sharp sound, the chains rattling. The cell inside was pitch black, and I conjured a sphere of light in the air so I could get a better look. The room was small, with no windows and no other doors. More chains were attached to the farthest wall, but otherwise the room was empty except for dust and dirt.

"It's perfect." I removed my cloak and handed it to him. "Chain me up, please."

The guard stared at me with his mouth hanging open. "Your majesty?"

Oren turned to the guard. "Give us a moment alone."

The guard nodded quickly, looking relieved as he darted away.

Oren frowned at me. "What is this all about?"

I clenched my jaw, but there was no way to hide this from Oren. I needed someone to make sure my orders were carried out, and Oren was the only person I trusted implicitly. "I've discovered what is terrorizing our kingdom and casting darkness across the land. Me."

Oren's frown deepened. "I don't follow."

I quickly told him everything that had happened last night and everything I'd pieced together. His face paled with each new part of the story.

"Are you sure about all this?" Oren asked. "Perhaps Rose saw wrong. Or maybe there's a better explanation, or..."

"I'm sure. The only solution is to lock me up every night, at least until we can find a better way to stop me or to end this curse."

He drew in a long breath as he stared at the prison cell beside us. "I don't like this, not one bit. But I'll do what you ask, for tonight at least."

"Tonight, and every night thereafter. As long as it takes until the kingdom is safe. You must promise me, Oren."

He scowled, but reluctantly nodded. "And what of the Queen?"

"She's gone, and I doubt she will return." Why did Oren have to bring her up? Thinking of her only brought more pain, especially knowing I might never see her again. It had only been a few hours, but I was already empty without her. I missed the way she made me feel, like there was more to life than darkness and grief.

"But—"

I held up a hand to stop him from mentioning her further. "Forget Rose. Find me some moonroot before the sun sets. It won't be long now."

"Yes, my lord." Oren gave me a reluctant bow, before departing.

Once he was gone, I entered the prison cell, making my way to the chains on the wall. Many of them were covered in rust, but they were thick and heavy. I only prayed they would be strong enough to hold me when night fell.

THIRTY-THREE

ROSE

We mourned for three days, and then the funeral ceremony was held at dawn the following morning. As the sun rose, the King's body was set alight on a pyre in front of the Sun and Moon temple, the same spot where I'd been married. I tried to forget that memory and focus on the priest's words as he droned on about what a great leader my father was, while smoke lifted his essence into the Celestial Lands. My sisters cried and Iris clutched my hand the entire time, but Lily stood apart from the rest of us. She looked like an ice sculpture, her face perfectly stoic and smooth, her back stiff and straight, her head high as it carried the weight of her icicle tiara, which would soon be traded for a crown. She was showing strength for her people, but I knew she was as distraught as the rest of us, if not more so. We could grieve openly, and though our lives would change as a result of this, none would change more than hers.

The rest of the day passed in a haze of food, formalities, and condolences, until the crowds finally dispersed and my sisters and I returned to our rooms, all of us exhausted. But before I could get any rest, I needed to check on Lily and make sure she was all right.

I found her in our father's study, sitting in front of his desk with her head bent as though she was listening to him lecture us, as he'd done many times before. I approached her from behind and wrapped my arms around her, resting my head against hers. She tensed as though I'd startled her, and then relaxed with a sigh.

"How are you doing?" I asked, as I moved to sit in the chair beside her.

"As well as I can be. Aunt Dahlia thinks we should do the coronation soon, but I can't even think about that right now." She stared down at her pale hands, which were clasped in her lap. "I always knew this day would come and I've spent my entire life preparing for it, but I still don't feel ready to be queen."

"I understand. Take as much time as you need. Don't let anyone rush you, but don't be afraid either. I know you'll be an amazing queen."

"Thank you." She offered me a weak smile. "That means a lot, since you're a queen now too."

I let out a short laugh. "Oh, trust me, you'll be much better at it than I am."

She tilted her head and studied me. "You seemed to be doing well when I saw you at the ball. Has something happened?"

"Raith and I..." I spread my hands, unsure how to explain without revealing anything about the threat to our land or Raith's hidden identity. "Things between us are complicated."

"I've heard that's true of every marriage. Is he still teaching you magic?"

"He is, but every time I make progress, he tries to hold me back."

She offered me a kind smile. "You can be a bit...headstrong."

I blew out a breath and leaned back in the chair. "So I'm told. All I want to do is help him and get close to him, but he always pushes me away. The last time I saw him we had a big fight. He said he didn't need me and doesn't love me, and I think he was lying, but it still hurt."

"What did you do after he said that?"

"I got the message about father then, so I teleported here immediately. I've been trying not to think about Raith ever since."

Her eyebrows darted up. "And how is that working for you?"

"Not that well," I said with a sigh. "I care about him more than I ever imagined I would."

"Then you should return to Ilidan soon and talk with him."

"I don't think he wants to see me. He told me to return here even before I knew about father." I tried to keep my voice from trembling, but it was difficult. "He doesn't want me in Ilidan anymore."

Lily reached across to cover my hand with hers. "Nonsense. He's lost so much, and he's built many walls around his heart. I barely know him and even I can see that. You're just the person to break them down, and I saw the way he looked at you during the ball. He cares about you more than you can imagine."

"Maybe you're right," I said, but my voice sounded defeated, even to me. "Have you had any luck finding anything related to Raith's first wife's death?"

Lily shook her head. "I looked through father's things, but didn't find anything about the assassination or a connection to Lord Malren. I'm sorry."

I waved a dismissive hand. "It's to be expected. If there was anything, I'm sure he destroyed it already. Our father was many things, but he wasn't stupid."

"You're welcome to take a look through his papers and see if you spot anything I missed." She stood slowly, like her bones ached. "As for me, I think I'll try to get some sleep."

We hugged once more, and then she left the room. As the door shut, I moved behind father's desk and sat in his chair, taking it all in. He'd sat here almost every day, plotting against Ilidan, finding ways to continue an unnecessary war. There had to be something in this desk connecting him and Malren, something tying them to Silena's murder. If I could only find it, maybe I'd be able to bring some peace to Raith's heart and find justice for Silena's death.

I opened each drawer of the desk and began going through Father's papers, searching for anything. If there was anything here it would have to be obscure or encoded, otherwise Lily would have found it already. The job was tedious, and my eyes quickly grew tired of reading small handwriting and faded words, but I kept going. I wouldn't give up, not until I'd found something or had gone through every scrap in this room.

When I was so tired I thought it would be a good idea to take a break and start again in the morning, I found a map of Ilidan with a small marking on it that caught my eye. The small X was on the eastern side of the kingdom, in a forest near a town called Bellsover. Why was that name so familiar?

I pinched the bridge of my nose, trying to focus despite the exhaustion sweeping over me. Bellsover, Bellsover... That was the town I'd teleported into looking for Raith. We'd fought back the shadow beasts there, which had come from a forest to the east. Why did my father have a map with that location on it? He would never be involved with magic or the Shadow Lord, so there must be some other explanation.

I searched my memory of that night. Raith hadn't wanted to investigate that area. He'd become cold and harsh the second I'd suggested it. Could this be where Silena was murdered? Was her death the start of all of this?

I had to return to Ilidan and find Raith. Not only because I loved him and wanted to do whatever it took to make our marriage work, but because he needed to see this map. It didn't prove that Malren was part of the conspiracy, but it might be the key to unlocking another secret—and ending the plague covering our lands and infecting Raith's heart.

I gathered the shadows to me, pictured home, and let the darkness take me there.

THIRTY-FOUR

ROSE

I teleported into Raith's study, which I guessed would be the most likely place to find him, but it was empty. He wouldn't be in his bedroom even at this late hour, so he must be in his workshop, unless he was out fighting the darkness... or causing it. I glanced out the window, fearing I might see his large shadowy form stalking across the gardens, but to my relief he wasn't there either.

When I stepped out of the room, cold dread ran down my spine. All the torches were extinguished, and the hallway was pitch black for the first time since I'd lived in the castle. I'd only been gone a few days, but something terrible must have happened in that time. I never should have left Raith alone here. I'd been so upset by his harsh words, and then my father's death had kept me in Talador, but I should have returned sooner or come back to check on

Raith, at least. He might have pushed me away, but I was his wife, and I should have been there for him.

I rushed through the dark castle, lighting torches with my magic along the way. I checked Raith's workshop, but it was as empty as his study. As were the hallways I ran through, which were completely devoid of guards or servants and as silent as a tomb. Shadowy tendrils reached out from the darkest corners, but retreated with each torch I lit. With every step my dread grew, along with my worry for Raith, Oren, and everyone else in the castle. Had they all fled in fear? Or had something much worse happened?

As I approached the entrance hall, inky darkness slithered along the ground, growing thicker the closer I got. One doorway was completely smothered by shadow, and I had to blast it with fire in order to get through. Soon it became impossible to light torches, as all the walls and ceilings were covered in the horrible, black muck. Out of the corner of my eye I glimpsed shadowy beasts darting about, slipping from one dark corner to the next. I summoned a ball of fire to protect me and light my way, but none of the creatures drew near.

Shouts outside urged me to move faster, and I clutched my skirts as I began to run toward the large doors leading to the front of the castle. One of them was open, the heavy stone bent in half and barely hanging from the hinges, as though something—or someone—had blasted through it. The darkness that dripped down the doorway gave me a good clue as to who.

I spotted Raith immediately when I emerged into the fresh night air. He towered over the courtyard in his shadowy form, his wings flaring wide as his clawed hand slapped at the soldiers waving torches at him. I gasped as he sent his own people flying, before inky ropes leaped from the ground to hold them down.

A man on a white horse yelled and raised his sword, ordering another group of soldiers forward. As his horse turned in my direction I realized it was Lord Malren, wearing golden ceremonial armor that looked more decorative than useful. What was he doing here?

As Raith swatted at Malren's guards, I sprinted down the steps, nearly tripping over my long skirts in my haste. I called out my husband's name, but my voice was lost in the wind and drowned out by the yells of the soldiers as they rallied against their king. Did they know it was him? Or did they think they were battling the true Shadow Lord? Either way, they must realize they didn't stand a chance against his magic. The only one who could stop him was me.

I blasted Raith back with a huge burst of fire aimed at his chest. As he staggered and the shadows reformed, I moved in front of the armed men and women, blocking them from the dark beast looming over us.

"Get back in the castle!" I called out to them, as I summoned a wall of fire between us and Raith. "Let me deal with this!"

"But, your majesty—" one of the soldiers protested.

"That is an order!" The longer they delayed, the more of

them that would get hurt. I had to somehow bring Raith back to himself—and I couldn't do that with these soldiers waving torches at him.

They hesitated, while Malren's white horse drew up beside me. "My queen, it is not safe for you here! Let my people handle this."

I was about to argue that he was the one in danger here, when Raith let out a menacing laugh and large, monstrous beasts made of shadow emerged behind him. Lord Malren ordered his guards to intercept them, while other soldiers who could still escape ran back to the relative safety of the castle. Many more were tied up in the thick darkness covering the ground around us, and I prayed they were still alive.

"Raith!" I cried out. "Stop this madness! These are your own people! This is your castle!"

"Yes, they are mine," his terrifying voice said, as he reached for his cousin. "And they shall pay for what they've done. Starting with Malren."

I hit his shadowy claws with fire, breaking up the darkness for a few seconds, enough time for Malren's horse to dart away. "No! This isn't you! Come back to me, Raith!"

Raith's crackling lightning eyes fixed on me. "There's no coming back now."

He suddenly vanished, along with the shadow beasts, though he left the rest of the darkness behind. I sighed and pinched the brow of my forehead as I gathered my wits, wondering what had changed in the last few days. From the moment I'd realized the truth about Raith I'd known he was dangerous, but he'd never attacked the castle before. He'd often been spotted lurking around outside of it, but had otherwise avoided coming closer...until now. Was this my fault? Was he punishing his people and his home because I'd left?

"He won't listen to reason." Oren stepped out from behind a pillar, and my heart twisted at the sight of him. One of his eyes was puffy and already turning black and blue, while his left arm hung limp, like he couldn't move it. "I fear the man we once knew is gone. Only the darkness remains."

"I don't believe that." I turned toward the castle to study the damage. Thick, tangible darkness had already covered half of it and continued to spread, smothering every doorway, window, and arch. Soon the entire castle would be completely lost. There was no way I could stop it by myself, but I could help the soldiers Raith had attacked.

I moved across the courtyard and freed each soldier from the darkness chaining them to the ground. I was relieved to see they were all still alive—proof that Raith wasn't as far gone as I'd worried.

Lord Malren's horse pulled up beside me while I released the last few prisoners, and he sheathed his sword. "I knew Raith was involved in this, but I had no idea it was this bad. He must be stopped."

Any hope I had of keeping Raith's dual nature a secret faded with Malren's words. He would never let Raith live this down. "I can stop him. I just need time."

"Maybe, maybe not. It doesn't matter either way. His days on the throne are over." He gave me a sadistic smile. "But don't worry, you can be my queen instead."

Disgust filled my mouth. I'd been unable to find anything linking him to Silena's death, but there was no doubt he was involved. "I will never be your queen. I'd rather be dead."

"A pity. I was hoping it wouldn't have to come to that."

I gave him a look of pure revulsion before walking away. I climbed the great black steps again and wiped sweat off my brow while I approached Oren. "Tell me how this happened."

The older man gazed down at the courtyard with despair. "After you left, Raith ordered us to lock him up every night in the most secure prison cell we had and told us to drug him with moonroot to inhibit his magic. It worked for the first few nights, but with you gone he retreated into himself as he did after Silena's death. Tonight he turned into that creature before he could take the moonroot, and he broke free. Sun and Moon help us all."

"This is my fault," I said, dragging a weary hand through my hair. "But I'll fix it, I promise."

"Don't blame yourself, Rose. You've done more to help Raith than anyone in years. Although if anyone can save him it's you."

"I'll find him, and I'll bring him back." I had a suspicion about where Raith had gone, remembering the thick X drawn on the map in the eastern part of the kingdom. But even if I'd had no idea, I'd still be able to find Raith anywhere in the world. He was my home, more than this castle or the one I'd left behind in Talador. All I had to do was close my eyes and reach for him.

THIRTY-FIVE

ROSE

When I opened my eyes, I stood in a dense, dark forest with trees covered in thick black sludge. It dripped from leaves and corrupted the ground around me, turning the land into a nightmarish scene. Shadowy creatures bared fangs at me from the branches and flew overhead, letting out shrill cries that made a shiver run across my skin. There was no hint that this had ever been a living forest—it had been completely overtaken by the darkness, probably some time ago.

Something large moved behind me, and I spun around to face the beast my husband had become. "Raith!"

"You do not belong here," his icy voice said. He towered over me, his shadowy wings flared wide, but didn't make a move to attack me.

"I belong wherever you are." I swallowed my fear as I took a step forward, confident he would never harm me.

Cold waves of darkness rolled off him and disappeared into the night, while his lightning eyes crackled with power. "You left me."

The rough pain in his voice broke my heart. "Only for a few days, and it was a mistake I won't make again. I'm here now and I'm not leaving, but I need you to return to me. Cast out the darkness and become the man I love once more."

He let out a haughty laugh. "That man is gone forever."

"He's not. He's still inside you." I took a step closer, hoping he would see the love in my eyes. "Come back to me, Raith. Please."

"No."

I bit my lip as I moved closer to him, trying to show I wasn't afraid, even though cold sweat dripped down my back. "I'm sorry I left. Oren brought me a letter from my sister telling me my father was gravely ill. When I teleported there, I discovered I was too late. My father was already gone." I bowed my head, the grief rising back to the surface, and my voice wavered with my next words. "I would have returned sooner if not for that, and I missed you terribly the entire time. Even after everything you said. And now..." I drew in a breath and reached for his clawed hand, but he pulled away. "Both my parents are gone, my sisters are far away, and I need you more than ever, Raith."

"Rose..." He bent over as if in pain and then the darkness folded in on itself, rushing back inside his body until my husband stood before me, fully human once again. He stumbled forward, and I caught him in my arms.

He looked up at me and lightly touched my face. "What are you doing here? I told you to leave me."

"And I ignored your order, as usual. I came back as soon as I could."

"I'm sorry about your father." He straightened up and pulled away from me. "But I wish you'd stayed away."

"You remember what happened while you were in your shadow form this time?"

"I do, unfortunately." He squeezed his eyes shut. "I tried to stop it. I tried to protect my people. But the darkness broke free, and now everyone knows the truth. The things I've done..." He shook his head, and his voice held so much agony it made my heart clench. "I should give up the throne."

"You will do no such thing." I propped my hands on my hips. "Ilidan needs you as its king, and that beast back there wasn't truly you."

"You're wrong," he said, his voice hollow. "It was me. All of it."

"I don't believe that, and the important thing is that I'm here now. Together we can break this curse, cast out the darkness, and make the kingdom safe again."

He scowled. "And how do you think we'll do that?"

"I'm not sure yet, but we'll figure something out. I know we can find a way to save you."

"Foolish girl. That's where you're wrong." He leaned forward, pinning me with his cold gaze. "I am made of shadows and ruin and nothing more. My heart is full of darkness, yet you wish to be its queen. You may think you can bring light to the dark corners of my soul, but you're wrong. There is no saving me. Not from this."

Once again he was trying to intimidate me and push me away, but I wouldn't have it anymore. I poked a finger at his chest, over his heart. The heart I knew wasn't as dark as he'd claimed. "No, you're the one who's wrong. I *am* your queen, and I *will* find a way to end this curse, because I am *never* giving up on you."

I took hold of his shirt and yanked him toward me, then slanted my mouth across his. He let out a low groan as he kissed me back, while his hands grasped my upper arms, his fingers digging into my skin. Passion unfurled between us, along with something more, something that bound us to one another, tying our fates together forever.

"You're the most infuriating woman," he said, as his hands moved up to slide into my hair, pulling my mouth back to his for another rough kiss.

"And you're the most impossible man."

"What a match we are." He gazed into my eyes, his thumb stroking my lower lip. "I love you, Rose."

My breath caught. "You do?"

"Sun and Moon help me, but I do."

Emotion filled my eyes with tears, and I couldn't stop the smile spreading across my lips. "I never thought I'd hear you say those words to me."

"And I never thought I would say them again." His breath rushed out of him, along with his confession. "The truth is, I've loved you from the first moment we met, when you tried to use that feeble spell against me. There was never any doubt I'd choose you as my wife and not one of your sisters. When I asked for volunteers, I knew you'd step forward. You're the only one I want, and though I've tried to fight it this entire time, I can't deny it any longer. When you left, I worried I'd lost you forever, just as I'd lost Silena. That's when I let the darkness take over. I couldn't fight it any longer."

I took his face in my hands. "You can still fight it, and now you'll have me beside you. Our magic is stronger together. And I love you too, more than I ever imagined."

"Rose—" he started, but then his body tensed, and a ragged cry escaped his throat.

"Raith!" I cried, clutching his arm. "What's happening?"

He looked at me with a tormented expression as darkness burst from his skin, smothering him in shadows. No, I couldn't let him turn into that beast again! I summoned spheres of light in my palms, but then I hesitated, worried I might hurt him. But as I watched, I realized the darkness was leaching from his skin, leaving his body and swirling high into the air. As the last of it left Raith, it gathered above us and then rushed east through the forest, streaking across the night sky.

When it was over, I studied Raith, but he didn't appear to be any different. "What was that?"

"I don't know." He smoothed a hand down his chest, and then looked up at me. "But I feel a lot...lighter. I think that shadowy part of myself is gone."

"How?"

He frowned. "I'm not sure."

I glanced east, where the forest was so thick with darkness it was hard to make out anything at all. "I think we need to follow it."

Raith's jaw clenched. "No. I can't."

"We're near where Silena died, aren't we?" I asked softly, causing him to look away sharply. "That's when you said all of this started, after her death. The darkness must be going there."

"I will not return to that place."

"It might be the only way to stop this. I'll be by your side the entire time. Together, we'll face whatever we find there."

He drew in a long breath and reluctantly nodded. It took him a moment to pull himself together, but then he stood tall and smoothed his hands over his black clothing, composing himself before setting forth toward the place where this all began—and where it would end tonight.

THIRTY-SIX

RAITH

The darkness covering the land grew thicker as we walked east, and it was hard to tell it had once been a forest and not a monstrosity made of shadow and gloom. Every instinct urged me to turn around and go back, but Rose's presence at my side kept me moving forward. She'd come back for me even after I'd pushed her away, and she'd faced me in my nightmarish beast form, ultimately bringing me back to myself. She had to be the most fearless woman I'd ever met, and my heart blazed with love for her. Admitting it out loud had been a great relief, and somehow it had cast the darkness from my soul at the same time.

We came to a smooth patch of land which must have once been a road, although now it looked more like a bubbling, oozing black river than anything else. I gazed down it's path and spotted something in the distance. Something moving...right where Silena had been killed. A dark blur that beckoned me forward, urging me to uncover its secrets.

I took Rose's hand and magic immediately sparked between us, giving me strength. We headed down the road, stepping in the few places the darkness had barely touched, while blasting anything back that blocked our way or reached for us.

I gripped Rose's hand tighter as we approached the place where my first wife had been murdered. I hadn't stepped foot in this area since I'd found Silena's body all those years ago. I'd sworn to never return, but now I had no choice. I had to face this part of my past, or I'd never be able to free my kingdom from this darkness.

As we approached the dark blur, memories of that night came rushing back to me. The carriage had been on its side, the horses bleeding out on the ground, and all the guards and servants dead around it. I'd rushed forward with dread gripping my heart, already knowing what I would find, but convinced I could stop it nonetheless. I'd yanked the carriage door open and found my beloved wife's body inside, her throat slashed open by an assassin's blade. I'd clutched her to my chest and roared with anger and despair, vowing to find whoever had done this to make them suffer like I did.

That was the last thing I'd remembered of that night. Until now.

In place of the carriage was a swirling black portal that leaked darkness across the land. A shadowy beast emerged as we drew closer, and I blasted it back with lightning.

There was no doubt this was the source of the darkness overtaking my kingdom.

"What is that?" Rose asked.

"A portal to the Shadow Lands." I truly was the cause of all this misery, even if my mind had blocked it from me all this time. But not anymore. Now the truth flooded my mind, too horrible to ignore any longer.

"How did it get here?"

"I made it." I stepped closer to the portal, staring into its shimmering dark depths. "I remember everything now. When I found Silena, the grief was so strong I lashed out with my magic and tore a hole to the Shadow Lands. The Shadow Lord appeared, the real one, and I begged him to give me the power to take vengeance on the people who had done this to her. He laughed and granted my wish, but not the way I wanted. He cursed me, twisting my magic against me, so that it would control me and turn me into a monster. The only way to break the curse was to allow my heart to love again, which he didn't think would ever happen."

Rose gasped. "Why would he do such a thing?"

"Because he was bored? Because he wanted to take over my land? Who can say for sure?" I turned toward her. "All I know is that you broke the curse. You showed me how to love again, and in doing so, you freed me of the darkness that had taken hold of my soul."

She squeezed my hand. "You're the one who truly broke the curse. You opened yourself to love a second time, even though you knew it might hurt you again."

"Only because you refused to let me continue on as the

miserable man I'd become. I couldn't have done it without you."

"All right, I'll admit I helped." She gave me a faint smile. "And just like we broke the curse together, we're going to close this portal together."

"It won't be easy. The Shadow Lord might resist us."

"We're two of the most powerful wizards in the world, and our magic is even stronger when we combine it. If anyone can do it, we can."

I brought her hand to my lips. "So confident and brave. You never let anything hold you back. That's why I love you." I fixed my eyes on the portal and steeled myself. "Now let's destroy this thing and end the plague over our kingdom once and for all."

She stared at me with a wondrous smile. "You said *our* kingdom."

"Of course I did. You're my queen."

Fiery determination lit up her eyes. "That's right, and I'm not stopping until all the darkness is gone from this land."

With our hands still linked, we turned toward the swirling dark portal and summoned runes for fire and lightning. Together we unleashed them upon the unholy gateway to the Shadow Lands, and it slowly began to shrink under our combined efforts. But the darkness wasn't letting go that easily. Monstrous shadow creatures emerged from the remains of the forest, flying and loping toward us at speeds no human could match. They let out horrid shrieks and cries, and when the first drew near, I turned to press my back against Rose's to face them while she continued attacking the portal.

"It's working!" Rose said, although her voice was strained with the effort of burning the portal with relentless fire.

"Don't stop!" I turned a shadow creature to ash with a blast of lightning. "No matter what happens!"

Dark tentacles suddenly reached out from the center of the portal and wrapped around us, burning us with icy cold malice. A menacing laugh filled the air, and then a cruel voice said, "You may have broken the curse, but I've already claimed much of your land. It's mine now."

I sent a wave of lightning through the tentacle, and it released me and shriveled away. "Never. This is our kingdom, and it shall never be yours. Be gone from this land forever."

"You can't stop me," the Shadow Lord said. An outline of a large man appeared in the blackness of the portal, but nothing more. "I am night itself, the space between stars, the silence between breaths. I existed long before you were even a distant thought, and I shall continue long after you're smoke and ash. None can defeat me."

"We can," Rose said, her fingers tightening around mine. She met my eye, and I nodded. For years I'd tried to stop the darkness alone, convinced I was the only one who could handle it. I told myself I didn't need or want any help. But I was wrong. Rose had shown me we were stronger together— and even if we failed, I would have no regrets.

We summoned magic together and it sparked between

our palms, growing stronger with the strength of our love. Fire and lightning combined before us and struck the portal as one, but the Shadow Lord lashed out with his dark magic and fought us back. It wouldn't be enough to stop him...but Rose and I both had a second affinity.

"We need to take control of the darkness!" I told her. "With me, now!"

I traced a rune in the air, confident Rose would be able to copy it. Her brow furrowed with concentration, but she managed to pull it off, and the darkness snapped into our control. The Shadow Lord roared and tried to regain control, but Rose and I held on, though sweat dripped down my forehead and she clenched her fists from the effort.

"Go back to the Shadow Lands!" I called out, as we sent the dark beasts and shadowy tendrils through the portal.

"This isn't over," the Shadow Lord said. "I am eternal. I will return for your daughter, and her child, and so forth, for however long it takes until this land is mine."

With those last haunting words, he vanished. The portal shrank in on itself and then disappeared. We stared at the empty space where it had once been, and then I turned to Rose and pulled her into my arms. We held each other for some time as the forest quieted once again, both of us exhausted from our hard-fought victory.

"It's over," I said, with a lightness I hadn't imagined I could ever feel. I clutched her face in my hands and kissed her, her soft lips banishing the last traces of darkness in my soul. "The curse is broken, and the kingdom is safe again."

For now, anyway. I wasn't sure what he'd meant about

our daughter—did he know something, or was he simply spouting ominous words to pretend he hadn't been defeated? Only time would tell.

Rose smiled up at me with love in her eyes. "I knew we could do it."

"I never should have doubted you."

I glanced back at the dark forest. Though the area around us had been cleaned of corruption, the rest was still covered in thick darkness, and shadowy beasts still roamed the land. It would take us some time to remove every last trace of the Shadow Lord's attack, but at least we'd put a stop to it.

Now it was time to return home and undo the damage I'd wrought there.

THIRTY-SEVEN

RAITH

When we returned Varlock Castle, my brief happiness was replaced by rage at the sight of Lord Malren. My cousin had been far too quick to arrive after I'd turned into that monster and escaped my prison, which meant he'd been waiting nearby for an excuse to ambush my home. Now that I knew he'd been involved in Silena's death, I wanted nothing more than to turn him to ash.

"I'd forgotten he was here," Rose said, her eyes narrowing. "I'm sorry, Raith. While I was in Talador I looked for evidence that Lord Malren and my father had conspired against you on the assassination plot, but I found nothing substantial."

"It doesn't matter," I growled. "I don't need proof."

I approached my cousin with my fists clenched while he ordered his guards to wave torches at my castle to fight back the darkness covering it. Guilt tore at me knowing I'd done that to my home, but the curse was broken now, and he had no business being here any longer.

At the sight of me, Lord Malren drew his sword dramatically. "Stay back, foul beast!"

I rolled my eyes. "Don't be ridiculous. This is my castle."

A haughty smirk lit up his face. "Not anymore. Not after what you did tonight."

"The curse has been broken and the Shadow Lord has been defeated," Rose said, making her voice loud so all the nearby soldiers and servants could hear it too, as they watched on with wary looks. "The threat to the kingdom is over."

"So you say," Malren drawled. "But how do we know you won't turn into that beast again tomorrow night?"

"You have my word," I said, gritting my teeth.

"Not good enough. The kingdom of Ilidan deserves a better king. Me."

I let out a harsh laugh and spread my arms. "If you think you can take my throne from me, I welcome you to try. It'll give me an excuse to send lightning through your bones until your insides cook and your eyes turn black." He hesitated, and I reached forward and wrapped my hand around his neck. "In fact, maybe I'll do that anyway. I know you were involved in Silena's death. It's time for you to pay."

"I wasn't!" Malren choked out. "You have no proof!"

"You told me as much at the ball," Rose said. "And made it clear you planned to do the same to Raith soon."

He glared at her. "I don't know what you're talking about, you crazy witch."

"Don't you dare speak to her!" My fingers tightened around his throat and sparks sizzled against his skin, making his eyes widen. His mouth fell open as he was shocked by the weak dose of lightning I sent through him. "I may not have proof, but I'm still king, and I'll make you pay for what you've done."

"Raith, no." Rose placed a hand on my arm. "Don't do this."

I stared into Malren's eyes as I gathered more lightning. "Why not? My dear cousin has no qualms about murdering me or my family. He deserves death for what he's done, and I'm more than happy to give it to him."

"Because you're not a monster like he is."

Wasn't I?

No, I realized. I wasn't. Not anymore. And not only because the curse had been broken, but because Rose had healed my dark, broken heart. As much as I wanted to make Malren pay, I wouldn't stoop to his level.

I released Malren, and he staggered back, clutching his throat. "Leave this kingdom and never return. If I catch even a hint of you in my lands again I'll hunt you down and continue what I started. And not even my lovely wife will be able to stop me then."

Malren gave me one last, glowering look before he scampered off to his horse. He jumped on it quickly and ordered his soldiers to follow, before darting off into the night.

"Thank you," I said to Rose. "Once again, you brought me back from the edge."

"All I did was help you find yourself." She stared after Malren with blazing eyes. "But it's a good thing he left, or I might have burned him alive myself."

I wrapped an arm around her. "I have no doubt, my fierce queen."

♛

We spent the rest of the night freeing the castle from the darkness that had covered it during my escape and apologizing to the soldiers who'd fought me and the servants I'd terrorized. Oren promised to send out a royal proclamation stating that the Shadow Lord had been defeated and the threat to the kingdom was over, after convincing me that no one else needed to know the truth about the beast who had stalked their lands and spread darkness across them. Guilt tore at my conscience, and I wasn't sure I would ever be able to make amends for what I'd done over the last few years, but as king it was my duty to try. At least I had my queen at my side to help me.

Once the castle was purged of darkness, Rose and I stumbled to my bedroom and collapsed into bed, too exhausted to do anything more than curl around each other as we drifted away. With my wife in my arms and the curse broken, I slept better than I had in ages. But when sunlight drifted past the curtains, I was coaxed awake by her light kisses on my neck and the soft curves of her body pressed against mine. She wore only a thin chemise, and I discovered it had ridden up during the night, allowing me to grab hold of her behind and tug her closer.

"Good, you're awake," she said, before pressing another kiss to my jaw.

"You seem to want something this morning," I murmured, as the last traces of sleep vanished.

She pushed back the blankets and her eyes roamed over my naked body. "I didn't get a chance to really look at you when we did this before. Or to touch you."

She smoothed a hand down my chest slowly, before dipping below my waist. She found me already hard for her, and she let out a little breathy gasp as her fingers circled my cock. I groaned as she stroked me up and down while admiring me like a new problem she wanted to solve. Her thumb moved over the head of my cock and I nearly went mad, especially from the way she looked at me with lust in her eyes. Lust that was surely reflected in my own.

I grabbed her thigh and hitched it up over mine, then moved my hand between her legs to find her entrance. She was already wet and so soft and inviting, especially when she moaned at my touch. Together we kissed and stroked each other until we were both delirious with need, and I knew if I didn't take her soon, I would surely go mad.

"Enough." I rolled onto my back and pulled her with me, forcing her to straddle my hips, and my cock slid inside her at the same time. She let out a delicious gasp as I filled her up completely, which I captured with my mouth. She kissed me back as our bodies joined together, only pulling apart when I grabbed her chemise to drag it over her head. With our naked skin pressed together I dug my fingers into her hips, wanting her as close as possible. Every inch of her was mine, now and forever.

I broke off the kiss to gaze into her eyes, which were hooded and heavy with desire. "Ride me," I commanded.

Her eyes widened, but she licked her lips in an enticing way and sat up. As her full breasts hung over my face, begging me to touch them, she began to roll her hips slowly. "Oh," she said, her voice heavy with pleasure. She did it again, slower this time.

"Yes, just like that." My fingers dug into her behind as I guided her to rock against me. "Find a rhythm that feels good."

"It all feels good." She took me deep inside her again and paused, closing her eyes as if savoring the moment.

I thrust into her hard. "I said, ride me."

She let out a short laugh. "When have I ever done what you told me?"

"Never," I admitted. "I don't know why I thought you'd start now."

She grinned down at me, but then began to do as I'd asked. Her breasts bounced as she moved, and I reached up to fondle them, my thumbs brushing against her hard nipples. She let out a moan and rode me faster, her eyes locked with mine the entire time. There was no better sight in the world than my beautiful wife taking her pleasure. Especially when she threw back her head and let her body take over, rocking harder and faster against me. I met her with steady, deep thrusts, giving her everything she demanded and more.

"Raith," she gasped, as her fingers curled into my chest and her eyes became wild.

"Chase it," I said, with a pinch of her nipples. "Take us both over the edge."

She cried out as she let go, and when she tightened and pulsed around me, I couldn't help but join her. I sat up to wrap her in my arms and hold her as we were both swept away by the intense pleasure. With our bodies pressed together we rode out the rest of the climax, clinging to each other the entire time.

"I love you," I said, as my heart pounded in time with hers.

Rose gave me the loveliest smile I'd ever seen as she touched my face in wonder. "I love you too."

I buried my face in her shoulder and breathed her in, feeling content for the first time in years. I never imagined I'd ever feel such love again, especially with the daughter of the man I'd hated for so long. I'd gone to Talador to end the war and had left with a bride I didn't want, who ended up changing my life forever. She'd released me from the curse that had consumed me and plagued my kingdom, and though I would always love Silena, I'd realized there was room in my heart for both of the women who had captured it. I could finally move on from my past, and let go of the darkness that had once consumed me.

Thanks to Rose, I was no longer a monster.

THIRTY-EIGHT

ROSE

TWO MONTHS LATER

A lingering shadow tendril reached out to wrap itself around my ankle. I seared it with a quick flash of fire, and it exploded into ash. Raith sent the darkness it had come from back to the Shadow Lands, and at last the town of Bristolen was free once more.

Raith and I had spent the past two months traveling around Ilidan to banish the darkness left behind after the curse was broken and the portal closed. Our tour of the kingdom had already done much to reassure our people, and it was a good way for me to meet them and to learn more about my new home too. There was still some hostility and pain left over from the war, and not everyone was kind or welcoming to me, but at least we'd begun the long process of healing and moving forward.

We'd cleared the inhabited towns first, where people had been living in fear, and then focused on the abandoned ones next. Bristolen had been completely smothered in darkness during the last year, but now people would be able to return to the town and rebuild their homes. Raith and I had promised funds, supplies, and soldiers to every town affected, which seemed to help relieve the guilt he felt about his involvement.

Bristolen was the last town on our list, and I was eager to return to Varlock Castle—especially since I had something to tell Raith. Something that filled me with giddy excitement, though I had no idea if he would feel the same.

"I think that's the last of it," Raith said, as he smoothed back his black hair, so handsome it took my breath away for a second. I loved him more with every passing day, and thanked the Sun and Moon for having him appear in front of me in the snow that afternoon. Raith often said I was the one who'd saved him, but in many ways he'd saved me too. I was no longer the unwanted princess secretly practicing magic, searching for a purpose while wishing she was anywhere but at her father's castle. Now I was a wife, a queen, and a wizard...and soon I would be something more.

"Shall we return home?" Raith asked, offering me his hand.

I took it with a smile. "Yes, supper is probably waiting for us already."

He pulled me close, wrapping his arms around me, and pressed a kiss to my neck. As he did, darkness surrounded us, whisking us away to the castle. When it receded, a wave of nausea swept over me as the magic faded. I pressed a hand to my stomach until it passed, focusing on breathing and not getting sick all over Raith. The queasiness had begun a few days ago and was growing stronger all the time, leaving little doubt in my mind as to my condition.

"Rose, is something wrong?" he asked, gazing at me with concern.

"No, not exactly." I drew back and smoothed my skirts. We'd arrived in the dining room, and the servants rushed in and began filling our glasses. I glanced at the wine and my stomach churned. It was time to tell Raith.

When the servants left the room, I took Raith's hand, preventing him from going to his chair. "Wait. There's something I need to tell you."

His brow furrowed. "What is it?"

"I..." I swallowed. "I believe I'm pregnant."

He blinked at me. "Truly?"

I nodded. "I haven't had my monthly courses in some time, and I've recently begun feeling quite sick and exhausted. I consulted with a midwife, and she agrees." I peered up at him, worried how he would take the news. Although an heir had always been in our plans for the future, we hadn't expected it to happen so soon, and he might not be ready yet. He'd barely gotten over Silena's death and everything that had happened with the Shadow Lord, and now he had this life-changing news dropped on him too.

Raith let out a surprised laugh and then gathered me in his arms, banishing all my worries with a kiss. He pulled back and studied my face, then glanced down at my stomach with a slight smile on his lips. "We're going to have a baby?"

"Yes, we are," I said, laughing softly. "Assuming all goes well, of course."

"It will. You're too stubborn to let anything happen to our child, and he or she will no doubt be the same."

"Or even worse," I said, giving him a playful nudge. "This baby will be half your child too, and you're just as stubborn as I am."

Oren walked into the room while Raith laughed. He'd recovered quickly from his injuries from that fateful night, and now his eyebrows darted up. "Is there something I should know about?"

Raith turned toward him, with one arm still wrapped around me. "Your wish has been granted, Oren. We've done our duty to the kingdom and an heir is on the way."

Oren clapped his hands together. "Oh, delightful! It has been far too long since the castle had any children running about. And having an heir will squash any lingering support of Lord Malren."

Raith's face soured at the mention of his cousin. Malren had left Ilidan after our encounter with him, but he was traveling through the other kingdoms and searching for allies so he could try to take the throne. Our spies reported that he hadn't found much success so far, but we were keeping many eyes on him anyway. As long as he was alive, he would be a thorn in our side, always causing trouble however he could. But I was still glad Raith hadn't killed him.

Oren cleared his throat and presented a scroll. "This arrived for you today from Talador."

I unfurled it, noting the ornate silvery script and the blue seal. "It's an invitation to Lily's coronation."

Raith glanced over the scroll, before handing it back to Oren. "Please let them know we will be there."

"Of course, your majesty." Oren gave us a quick bow and left the room.

"Your sister is going to make a fine queen," Raith said, as we took our seats.

"Yes, she is. And instead of being enemies, Talador and Ilidan will be allies for the first time in decades."

Raith reached across the table to take my hand and pressed a kiss to my knuckles. "We're going to leave behind a legacy of peace and prosperity, instead of war and death. And it's all because of you."

"And you," I said, smiling at him. "You started all of this by having the courage to try to end the war in the first place."

"True, but I couldn't have done it without you." He raised his glass of wine and took a sip, then shook his head. "An alliance between Talador and Ilidan. Who could have guessed such a thing would ever happen in our lifetime?"

"My mother knew." She'd foreseen that Lily and I would both be queens and that we were going to change the world together. Now we had that chance, and it was time for us to move past the sins of our parents and find a way to correct their mistakes. Lily and I would be the start of a new peace between our kingdoms, and though I didn't have the gift of prophecy like my mother, I knew in my gut that my other sisters had important destinies ahead of them too. The six of us were going to reshape the entire world, forging new kingdoms built on love and prosperity instead of hatred and war, so that when the next generation took the throne, they'd be proud of what we'd done. I rested my hand on my stomach and smiled at the thought.

Raith covered my hand with his own larger one, and our eyes met as our combined magic jumped to life. I searched his handsome face for any lingering darkness, but found none.

The beast that had once consumed him was gone, and only love remained.

ABOUT THE AUTHOR

New York Times Bestselling Author Elizabeth Briggs writes unputdownable romance across genres with bold heroines and fearless heroes. She graduated from UCLA with a degree in Sociology and has worked for an international law firm, mentored teens in writing, and volunteered with dog rescue groups. Now she's a full-time geek who lives in Los Angeles with her family and a pack of fluffy dogs.

Visit Elizabeth's website: www.elizabethbriggs.net

Made in the USA
San Bernardino, CA
02 February 2020